PROLOGUE

Cathy lifted the latch. The gate swung inward. Up ahead a squirrel darted across the trail, quickly vanishing into the pine trees that lined both sides.

Rebecca, Cathy's best friend, pulled the gate closed and relatched it. "What do you want to do for your big four-o?" she asked.

"Hot dogs," Cathy said. "With chili, cheese, and onion. Lots of onion."

Her friend gagged.

They laughed.

"Well, how about we start with this." Rebecca slid her hand into the deep pocket of her baggy jeans. She brought out a stained and scuffed ring box. Cathy gasped.

"Now don't get too excited," Rebecca said. "I made it."

Cathy grabbed the box. She cradled it to her chest, rocking it. "I'll love it. I promise!"

"Maybe you should look at it first before you make any promises." Rebecca smiled.

Cathy opened the box. Inside rested a ring with three

silver wires twined together, holding a blue moonstone in place. "That's my birthstone!"

"I know, you goofball." Playfully, Rebecca punched her. "Try it on."

Eagerly, Cathy did, sliding it onto her middle finger. It was perfect. She hugged her friend's shoulders, hard. "Thank you. This means the world to me."

"You are very welcome." Rebecca squeezed her back.

They each wore large well-worn backpacks—a burgundy one for Rebecca and a blue one for Cathy—filled with everything they owned. Cathy always joked that Rebecca's pack weighed more than she did.

The friends fell in step along the trail that cut through Memorial Gardens. With a Zippo lighter, Cathy lit a cigarette.

Rebecca crinkled her nose. "Those'll kill you," she said, as she always did.

Cathy took a drag anyway.

They'd been in Iris, Tennessee, a few months now.

Miles of open trails! Forestry! Grand Smoky Mountain views!

That's what the city's website said. All Cathy knew was that she liked it a whole lot better than many of the other towns where they'd taken up living.

Between Francis House, the local shelter, and Tent City, the encampment out in the country, they made provisions for the homeless here.

Plus, her daughter was here.

She was the last person Cathy expected to see. It had been ten years. Her daughter had grown into a young woman, but she instantly knew her face. Cathy had been waiting in line at Francis House for a hot meal and hopefully a cot when she walked right out the door, past Cathy,

UNSEEN

NELL BRACH, BOOK TWO

S. E. GREEN

and on down the sidewalk where she climbed into a van and drove away.

Cathy had stood frozen, unable to believe it.

"You look like you saw a ghost," Rebecca had said.

"I-I just saw my daughter!" Cathy had been so excited, she shouted the words. Everyone in line had turned.

That had been four weeks ago now and Cathy hadn't seen her daughter since. She'd asked around, but no one knew who the young woman was. Cathy began to wonder if it had all been in her mind.

Off to the right, a water tower glinted in the setting September sun. Beyond that, a paper factory whispered with activity.

Side by side the friends continued walking, rounding the curve in the trail. Cathy had been living a couple of years on the streets when she met Rebecca, who was older by ten years and took on a protective big sister role. They instantly became friends and had been that way since. Knowing someone had your back was the key to surviving this life of theirs.

The bordering trees came alive with chirping birds and the sound of small animals scurrying through pine needles. Up ahead two squirrels chased each other. Overhead, one lone bird coasted on the warm breeze.

Cathy paused to pick up a stick. She swished it through the air like a sword. Her mood dipped. What would her daughter's reaction be upon seeing Cathy again? Would she remember her? *Of course, she would,* Cathy silently admonished herself. But would she recognize Cathy was an entirely different question. Ten years of living on the streets had not been kind to her. She looked nothing like the woman she used to be.

Maybe Cathy should stop asking around about her and

leave things be. They both had moved on. It wasn't like she had thought of her daughter every day or even every week. She thought of her now and then, though, wondering where she was, what she was doing, and what she looked like now.

"You're suddenly very quiet. Anything wrong?" Rebecca asked.

"Just thinking about my daughter," Cathy said.

"No luck finding her?"

"Nope. She wore khaki pants, a navy top, a white ball cap, and climbed into a van. That's all I've got."

"There are a lot of vans that come and go from Francis House."

"I know," Cathy sighed.

Just then a siren went off in the distance at the paper mill. A large plume of dark smoke billowed into the sky. Rebecca turned to look.

Taking one last drag of her cigarette, Cathy paused to grind it out on the sole of her tennis shoe before tucking the butt into the front pocket of her yellow shorts. "Gotta do a number two." She cut off the trail into the woods.

Behind her, Rebecca continued walking. "Meet you at the end."

The end of the trail wasn't far, and Cathy waved as she disappeared into the pines. A few yards in, the scent of a skunk had her backtracking. She stepped back onto the trail, now seeing Rebecca further up, and crossed over, disappearing into the other side.

She went further in than needed. It wasn't like either one of them was in a hurry. Plus, she wanted to think. She found a downed tree with a natural hole where the limbs separated and came back together. She placed her backpack to the side, lowered her elastic-banded shorts and underwear, and gave a little hop to get up. Her shorts gathered around her ankles. Her shoes barely touched the ground.

As Cathy sat over the hole, she looked out over a leaf-covered gulley that dipped and then climbed back up.

Idly, she wondered if her poop would roll down into that gulley.

Further out more trees spread over several acres of the nationally protected forest. She'd heard some Civil War fight occurred here. Other than the trail, there was nothing to Memorial Gardens but acres of pine trees. There certainly weren't any gardens.

Cathy had gotten used to this life. She couldn't imagine resuming a "normal" one.

Nothing moved in the forest. No sound came—not even the birds and squirrels. Just one minute ago, they were so active.

Overhead the late summer sun shifted, about to set. The canopy of leaves and branches cast the area with shadows. Soon this area would be dark.

Her feet dangled from her perch. She swung them back and forth, sifting through the fallen pine needles.

She began humming a song she hadn't thought of since her daughter was a baby. The humming turned to soft singing. The soft singing became louder. She laughed. She couldn't remember the last time she belted out a tune.

Cathy closed her eyes and began again.

If she hadn't been singing, she would have heard the footsteps.

If she hadn't had her eyes closed, she would have seen the shadow.

If she hadn't had her shorts down, she might have been able to run.

ONE

Monday, 11 a.m.

IN SHERIFF OWENS' office, I stand beside my partner, Detective Vaughn London, watching the video filmed three weeks ago at a maximum security facility in Knoxville.

"Rylan Scott, this death warrant orders your execution in thirty days for the crime of murder in the first degree of Paige Bell. You will be relocated to the intensive management unit and placed on death watch for the duration of your incarceration. Your attorney has been provided with the same forms and documentation."

Rylan Scott. That name is vaguely familiar.

"Do you understand everything I just told you?" the government official asks.

The inmate, dressed in orange and with a shaved head, nods.

"Do you have any questions?"

"No." The inmate shakes his head. "But I'd like to see Detective Nell Brach, if possible."

The video ends.

Surprised, I look at Sheriff Owens.

"Thirty days. That's this Friday," Vaughn says. "He's being executed at the end of the week."

"Why me?" I ask. "And why am I just now seeing this?"

"There were some hang-ups with the request, but it's finally been approved and left to your discretion," Sheriff Owens says. "You can ignore it, or you can go. This only landed in my inbox this morning. It's the first I'm hearing of it as well, though I did review this." The sheriff hands me a folder. "Rylan Scott violently stabbed his sister-in-law to death and left her alone to bleed out on the kitchen floor of the apartment he shared with his wife and daughter. The murder weapon was found in his truck, covered in her blood. Unbeknownst to Rylan, his young daughter was in the bathroom. She saw everything. The little girl remained hidden. In the end, it was Rylan who ended up calling nine-one-one. However, it was the cops who found the little girl hiding in the bathroom."

"What about the mother?" I ask.

"Gone. She was partying with friends. Stumbled home days later only to discover her husband had been arrested for killing her sister and that her little girl had been placed in foster care. After giving a statement, she signed over rights and left."

I blink. "Rights to her daughter?"

"That's what the file says." He nods to it. "When you look at that, you'll see the mother and sister are identical twins. It's believed Rylan thought he was stabbing his wife, not her sister. Only afterward did he realize it was the wrong twin, had an attack of conscience, came back, and dialed emergency. Your grandfather was good friends with the lead investigator and asked to consult on the case. From what I can tell, your grandfather did not believe Rylan Scott was guilty. Though the specifics on that aren't clear."

The sheriff checks his phone, then excuses himself, leaving me and Vaughn in his office.

I open the folder. Rylan Scott's mug shot greets me. Unlike the video, in the mug shot he has shaggy brown hair and a full beard. He's also ten years younger, putting him at thirty-five in this photo. Next, I see the shot of Paige Bell sprawled on her stomach across the yellow kitchen linoleum. Blood soaks her oversized T-shirt, pooling on the floor beneath. The stab marks are chaotic, done in an angry frenzy, starting in the front and then switching to her back as she tried to crawl away.

Nineteen in all.

Jesus.

Next, I look at the photos of the twin sister and her daughter. With dark features and pretty olive skin, the sisters are most definitely identical. The daughter's lighter, favoring the father.

I hand the folder to Vaughn who's been eagerly waiting. Today he wears a psychedelic paisley tie that makes me wince. We've been working together for five months now and I don't think I've seen the same tie twice. He told me they were meant to disarm people. It works. People—including me—do tend to stare at them.

"Thoughts?" he asks, flipping through.

"I'm no twin expert, but I find it hard to believe a husband mistakes a wife to the extent that he kills the wrong sister. Also, if the wife was gone partying for days on end, it couldn't be the first time. Where did Rylan think his daughter was, if not in the bathroom? And what killer stashes the blood-soaked weapon in his own vehicle? Not to mention coming back to the scene *and* calling it in? Don't even get me started on the mother signing over the daughter to the system. What the hell?"

"I don't know who the woman is but I already don't like her," Vaughn adds.

My phone buzzes with a text. It's Grace, my best friend.

Grace: Just a friendly reminder that you have a commitment.

Me: Believe me, I didn't forget.

"I took the afternoon off." I show Vaughn my phone. "My 'family obligation' awaits."

He winces. "Good luck."

"More importantly, good luck to you. Your sergeant's exam is today. How do you feel?"

"Nervous. Ready."

"You got this."

"You do realize if I pass I'll outrank you, which means I get to boss you around."

My eyes narrow. "Just try. And it's not *if* you pass, it's *when*."

Outside the sheriff's office, our newest hire in charge of domestic violence, Sergeant Chris Rogers, laughs loudly. "I told you I'd kick your ass at golf. Y'all don't believe this country boy can swing!"

"That guy gets on my nerves," Vaughn mumbles.

"Yep."

TWO

Monday, 12:15 p.m.

WHEN I ARRIVE at City Park, my favorite running spot, everyone is already here. There's my family—Tyler, Mom, Dad—and Mom's best friend Olivia's family—Luca, Grace, her husband Matthew, and their kids.

It's been five months since Dad re-entered our lives. Why am I the only one less than thrilled? Mom, as usual, welcomed him right in like he hadn't been absent during my entire childhood, Tyler's as well, and during her incarceration. Tyler followed suit, quickly forming a bond. Olivia watches for Mom's cues, then jumps in, as a best friend should. The only one sort of on my side is Grace, who is currently walking toward me.

Dressed in a white sundress and with her youngest on her hip, she smiles prettily and waves. "I was wondering when you'd show."

I close the door of my white Ford Interceptor and slide my new aviators on as I survey the gathering. Matthew's manning the grill. Tyler and Dad are tossing a football. Mom and Olivia are sitting at the picnic table drinking lemonade. Luca's under a tree scrolling his phone. And Grace and Matthew's two oldest are chasing each other.

The all-American summer family cookout.

Once upon a time, Luca would've been tossing the football with them, but he and Tyler still do not get along. I no longer worry about it. Luca crossed a line with Tyler. My brother has every right to be upset. I didn't tell Mom or Olivia about what Luca did to Tyler at school, but I had a good old-fashioned talk with Luca. A come-to-Jesus discussion as my grandfather would have said.

There is nothing wrong with healthy fear. Luca now has that with me.

Grace's youngest, now nine months old, reaches for me and I happily take her. "Oof, she's getting heavy."

Grace laughs. "Of the three, she's my biggest eater."

I tickle her chubby belly. She smiles and giggles. "Okay, that's about the best sound ever."

With a sigh, Grace looks over at our families. "What do you think the 'big announcement' is?"

"I don't know. If I had to wager, I'd say Dad's moving here from Georgia. All this back-and-forth he's been doing has got to be tiring. All I know is, he's not moving in with me and Tyler. He's getting his own place."

Slowly, we walk from the parking lot toward our families. The park is full today of everyone doing what we're doing—family picnics, softball, football, playground activities, and people hiking the trails.

Grace asks, "If he does relocate here, do you think your mom will move out of my mom's place and in with him?"

"Yes, in a heartbeat."

Mom and Olivia glance up as we approach. Mom

smiles widely. It's a good and happy smile. I'm pleased to see it, but I can't stand the fact Dad's the one who has put it there. He's going to break her heart, just like he has done countless times over the years, and I'm going to be the one to pick up the pieces. Only this time it won't just be her, it'll be Tyler as well.

The baby squirms in my arms. I'm just about to hand her off when she chooses to snuggle in, tucking her head against my chest. I press a kiss on her soft red hair. Guess she's going to be here a while.

Grace rubs her back. "If she gets heavy, just hand her off."

"I'm good. It'll be my core strengthening for the day."

"Or more like a lower back workout."

Tyler catches sight of me and waves. I wave back.

Matthew announces loudly, "Okay, I've got hot dogs, burgers, and barbecue drumettes. Who wants what?"

THIRTY MINUTES later everyone is either sitting or standing around the picnic table finishing the last bites of our cookout. I drag my remaining drumette through mustard and eat it as I throw my paper plate away.

Standing, Dad clears his throat. He smiles at Mom and she nervously gets up from the picnic table to stand beside him. He's six-four and she's five-three. Their size difference never seems dramatic until they're right next to each other. Tyler and I get our height from him, but we get our light hair and brown eyes from Mom.

"Thank you all for coming." Dad puts an arm around Mom. "We have exciting news and you are the people we want to share it with, our family."

Dad casts a glance at me. I fold my arms and behind my aviators, I stare at him. He clears his throat. Good, I'm glad I make him nervous.

"First, let me start by saying how humbled I am that you have welcomed me with open arms. I'm fully aware I don't have the best track record as a father. But I aim to change that. I'm finally at a spot where I make a good living, I've got a nice home, and I want to build a future full of promise and family." He smiles lovingly at Mom.

He continues, "For five months now I've been traveling back and forth from Georgia nearly every weekend." He looks at Tyler. "I've loved every minute of getting to know my brave, talented, intelligent son."

Tyler grins.

"I've loved every minute of my time with Jill." His arm around Mom tightens. Her cheeks flush under the attention. "And I'm slowly getting to know Nell again." He looks at me.

No, he's not. What the hell does that mean? I barely speak to the man.

He laughs. "It's taken me a long time to get to this place in my life. I know who I am and what I want. And what I want is my family. So, I asked Jill to marry me, and she said yes!"

Tyler woots.

Mom laughs.

Olivia jumps up.

Grace smiles.

Dad picks Mom up and swings her around.

Matthew squeezes Grace.

Their daughters dance around my parents.

Luca goes back to looking at his phone.

And I stay right here by the garbage can, numb. This is not good news.

———

I NOW STAND PROPPED against my vehicle, watching everyone clean up from the family picnic. Mom's been glued to Dad's side ever since the big announcement.

Questions. I have so many questions.

Is Dad moving here?

Is Mom moving there?

Has Mom checked with her probation officer?

What about Tyler? I'm his legal guardian. They can't just decide to take him. Surely, they know that.

What about Grandpa's house that I live in? Technically it belongs to Mom, but she hates that place. There are too many bad memories linked to it—a horrible relationship with my grandfather, a mother who abandoned her, and we had just moved in when Tyler was taken.

Plus, what about Tyler's private online school? He's thriving in that environment. It was a good decision to enroll him. Hell, if Dad wants to help so much why hasn't he offered to pay Tyler's tuition? It's not exactly cheap.

A shadow falls over me. I glance up to see my brother quietly approaching. He takes the spot beside me.

"You okay?" he asks.

"Of course."

"I know your 'deep thought' face and you're definitely in it."

I focus on changing that face—whatever my "deep thought" looks like—into a pleasant one. "It's a lot. That's all. I wasn't expecting an engagement announcement." Though I suppose that's a better one than, *We eloped!*

But isn't every child supposed to be excited their parents are getting married?

"I sort of saw it coming," he says.

I want to ask him all the questions running through my brain, but they need to be directed to Mom.

Tyler nudges me with his shoulder. "I love you."

"I love you too." I hug him.

"I won't leave you," he whispers. "If that's what you're worried about."

My heart melts. My arms around him tighten. My brother is my whole world. My feelings on this aside, this is about what's best for Tyler.

I need to sit down with both Mom *and* Dad and discuss what this means. Sooner rather than later, because this is the kind of shit that eats me up.

I should also find a family lawyer. I have a feeling I'm going to need one.

THREE

I STAND at the open door of my grandfather's shed. For the most part, I haven't done anything with this in the years I've lived here. His old tools and hunting gear line the shelves to the left. In the center is a dusty foldable table with two chairs. On the right are cardboard file boxes containing his research on long ago cases—both solved and unsolved.

I knew the name Rylan Scott sounded familiar. He's in one of these boxes. I just have to figure out which one.

It only takes me fifteen minutes of searching to find what I'm looking for. Sheriff Owens gave me a file on Rylan Scott, sure, but this one here in the shed will have more.

After wiping off the table, I sit down and open Grandpa's version of things. There are many of the same items—pictures, lab results, forensics, investigative notes—but other things as well.

There's a thick paper with giant black X's drawn in

crayon over and over again in rows; contact information on a foster home the girl was placed in; and papers legally changing the girl's name, though her new name has been redacted.

I jot down the number of the foster home, located in Knoxville. Then I scan a few notes, scrawled in my grandfather's slanted writing:

- *No prints on the murder weapon*
- *Unreliable witness—traumatized, mute, unable to recall details*
- *Alibi?*
- *DNA present due to Rylan's efforts*
- *Wife's questionable life*
- *No forced entry*
- *Tattoo...?*

Quickly, I thumb through the rest of the pages, but I don't see any mention of the mother who signed over rights. Other than her notated name, Natalie Scott, and the statement she made, there's nothing else. It's like she disappeared. She's a ghost.

Why run? Why sign over rights? Was she scared, or did she see an opportunity to finally be untethered?

Back to the little girl. Her name was Mackenzie Scott. Why did my grandfather facilitate changing it? Why redact it from a personal file? Was he concerned someone would find this file? Was he worried for the girl's life? Or was he trying to give her a clean slate with a new future?

The lead investigator on the case was Captain Joe Bacote. I know him. Or rather I met him a couple of times. Sheriff Owens was right. My grandfather and Captain Bacote were longtime friends. They used to go hunting together. The last time I saw or talked to Captain Bacote was years ago at my grandfather's funeral.

Did Captain Bacote's thoughts on the case align with my grandfather's?

I'm about to dial the number to the foster home where the little girl was placed when my phone buzzes with a group text:

Sheriff Owens: Nell, I realize you have the afternoon off but I need both of you at Memorial Gardens ASAP.

Vaughn: I just finished my exam. I'll be there soon.

Me: Me too.

Sheriff Owens: We've got a body.

FOUR

MEMORIAL GARDENS TAKES up a good portion of Iris, a town that butts up to White Quail and is home to our county's paper mill. Vaughn's Mini Cooper is already here when I pull up, plus Sheriff Owens' car, an ambulance, two squad cars, and the county forensics van.

A gate stands open, leading onto a long and winding trail bordered on both sides by thick pines. Halfway down the path stands a uniformed officer and a man with his dog, both looking off to the left where I assume everyone is.

In the distance, the paper mill's stacks emit white billowing clouds. A nearby water tower glows brightly in the sun with IRIS painted in giant letters.

Some minutes later I come up next to the officer.

She nods in the direction they were looking. "About fifty yards in. It's bad. Brace yourself."

"You found the body?" I ask the man.

"M-my dog did."

I look into his anxious eyes. "What's your name?"

He has to think about that. Poor guy's in shock. "Fred Gentry."

"Nice to meet you, Mr. Gentry. We're going to need you to stay around for questions. I'm going to have Officer Franks escort you from the trail to wait. Okay?"

He nods.

I let the black lab sniff my hand, before rubbing its head. When they're down the trail several paces, I move into the woods. Almost instantly the air around me stills like the animals and bugs know something is wrong. My hiking shoes sift through dry underbrush, producing the only sound.

As I shift around a tree and duck under a low-hanging branch, the back of Vaughn comes into view. He stands next to Sheriff Owens looking down into a gulley where county forensics is currently taking pictures.

I step up next to them. A heavy-set woman with short salt and pepper hair lies facedown partially buried by dirt and leaves. Her yellow shorts and white underwear are pushed down, gathering around her ankles and exposing her butt and the back of her legs. She wears a large white tee shirt, soaked with blood and shredded from the stab marks.

So many marks.

Vicious ones with no pattern. Angry stabs that drive deep into the fleshy fat of her back, arms, and butt. Her head rests at a cocked angle, and her jaw is hinged open as if she'd been in the middle of a scream.

A few feet from her body is a backpack that's been charred, inside and out, with the igniter fluid left beside it.

Letting the camera dangle around his neck, the forensic tech uses a brush to remove debris, fully exposing the woman's body. He pauses, leaning in to study her dirty face. Only, I don't think it's dirt. I can't tell from here, but there is something wrong with her skin. It looks like someone used that lighter fluid on her as well. The tech probes inside of her mouth. He moves down her body picking up one hand to inspect the fingers.

He looks up at the three of us. "Whoever did this didn't want us to identify her. The killer burned her face and fingers and pulled her teeth." A silver object next to her head catches my attention. It's partially buried, but the tech sees it also. He picks it up. It's a Zippo lighter. He shows it to us, nodding to the igniter fluid. "Let's hope it happened post-mortem."

"How long has she been here?" The sheriff steps down into the gulley.

"Almost twenty-four hours."

A mosquito lands on my neck. I swat it. "She was trying to get away and the killer kept slashing her."

"I was just thinking that." Taking his Ray-Bans off, Vaughn follows the sheriff down to the body.

I stay where I am, analyzing the area around her. The gulley's about twenty feet long and ten feet wide, dipping down roughly six feet before climbing back up to the edge. Over to the right, I note a different pattern in the leaves and pine needles. They're not haphazardly scattered as is usual for a forest. They're matted, exposing dirt underneath, almost like a trail.

I walk the edge around to that spot, coming to a stop at a downed tree. Two sizable limbs separate and come back together, forming a hole. Directly under that part is a dried pile of human feces. Blood slashes the bark.

"She wasn't raped," I say. "She was sitting right here going to the bathroom. The killer attacked. She fell forward, tumbling down into the gulley. The killer followed, continuing to stab until she finally stopped crawling away."

Wearing latex gloves, Vaughn slides a crumpled piece of paper from the pocket of her shorts. It's thin and waxy, like the type you wrap sandwiches in. He points to a torn burgundy sticker. "Francis House."

"That's the homeless shelter."

FIVE

Monday, 7 p.m.

TWO-STORY AND WHITE BRICK, Francis House was originally a sewing factory that went out of business. It sat empty for decades until one of the local churches bought it and made it into a shelter that has provided services for men and women going on ten years now.

A few people gather on the sidewalk in front. As I bypass them without saying a word, Vaughn nods to each person and greets them with a pleasant *Hello* and *How are you* and *Pretty evening tonight, huh?*

I try the knob on the red metal door, finding it locked, and ring the bell.

A moment later, it opens. An average-sized man with dark hair and a neatly trimmed beard smiles. I'd place him in his early thirties. "Yes?"

Simultaneously we flash our badges and introduce ourselves.

"Are you the person in charge?" I ask.

"I am. Everyone calls me Preacher Mitch."

"We need to ask you a few questions," I say.

"Of course. Come on in."

We step into a small entryway that leads down into a large room sectioned off by dividers, creating an eating area, a sleeping space for men, one for women, and a lounge with a TV and board games. About twenty people are here producing a slight buzz of conversation. Two women with hair nets circle the tables, refilling glasses or picking up garbage.

"We're just wrapping dinner," Preacher Mitch says. He points down a hall. "My office is down there."

I trail behind, peeking in and out of open doors. Boxes fill most of the rooms with clothes and toiletries and canned and boxed food. At the end of the hall, we enter a well-organized and clean office with a desk and laptop, multiple filing cabinets, and a corkboard filled with pictures.

While I look at the pictures, Vaughn holds up an evidence bag with the wax paper stamped Francis House. "Do you recognize this?"

"Yes, we wrap sandwiches in it. They go in our bagged lunches."

"Do you keep a record of who you give bagged lunches to?" Vaughn asks.

"No. That's one of the benefits of Francis House. We don't ask questions. We offer refuge for those in need. As long as they follow our one rule, they're allowed through our doors."

"And that rule is?"

"Respect one another. Simple enough. Will you tell me what this is about?"

"We found this on a dead body," Vaughn says. "We're trying to identify the woman."

Preacher Mitch becomes silent.

I turn from the photos to look at him. I'm surprised to see so much pain on his face for a woman we haven't even identified.

"Where?" he asks, his voice quiet and reverent.

"Memorial Gardens," I tell him.

He nods.

"How long have you worked here?" I ask.

"Only six months."

"Do you know the regulars fairly well?"

"I do."

I tap a photo of two women, both Caucasian, one light-skinned and skinny with long medium brown hair, the other olive-toned and heavy with short salt and pepper hair. Sitting beside each other on one of the cots out in the main room, they smile for the camera.

"Who are these two?" I ask.

"That's Rebecca and Cathy."

Vaughn steps up beside me. I point to Cathy with the short hair. He nods.

"When was the last time you saw them?" I ask.

"They were both here last night for an early dinner. They said they were coming back, but neither one did. That's not unusual, though."

I take the picture from the corkboard. "Where do they go if they don't sleep here?"

"Usually Tent City or the Iris Motel. Of the two, I try to steer them toward Tent City."

"Why is that?" Vaughn asks.

"Because the Iris Motel is disgusting. Sure they get a

bed, a shower, and a meal, but Gilda—she's the owner—always expects something in return."

I give Preacher Mitch my card. "If you see either one, call me."

SIX

Monday, 7:45 p.m.

TENT CITY IS out in the country, almost to the county line. Iris Motel sits next to the interstate, putting it closer to where we currently are. We opt to go there.

On the way, I dial Tyler.

"I'm good," he says by way of answering the phone.

"You sure? It's past my usual time getting home."

"Dad and Mom are here. We're playing Monopoly."

I love that he sounds happy, but it annoys the hell out of me that our father is part of that. "Okay, see you soon."

We hang up.

I glance at Vaughn. "I won't have time for Tent City."

"All good."

It only takes us ten minutes to go from Francis House out to the interstate.

One-story and L-shaped with twelve total units and the office in the center, only a few of the exterior lights work.

And even those are on their last flickering breath. It has a rent-by-the-hour type of feel to it.

Which it is.

I've driven past here many times, not paying it much mind. With trees surrounding it and a service road behind it, the Iris Motel is the only thing on this tiny off-ramp. A few miles down the service road will take you to the next exit full of fast food and better lodging.

I pull in and park next to a semitruck. My lights hit the window of Room 2 where the heavy curtains stand open, showing a woman on her knees giving a man a blowjob. Neither of them glances up at my intrusion. I turn my lights off, giving them privacy. Not that they care.

We climb out.

As we cross the cracked parking lot, I note only one other vehicle parked at the end. It's an old white Chevy with four doors. Probably belongs to the owner.

I survey the rooms, all with heavy dark curtains—some open, some closed. Stains trail the exterior brick and wood. The roof dips in several locations. The rusted gutter breaks away above Room 5. The place needs power washing. Or bulldozing.

"Not exactly where you bring your prom date to," Vaughn says.

I shrug. "I don't know. I might have put out if my date brought me here."

My partner laughs.

He opens the office door. We step inside a small area smelling of mildew. Behind a counter smudged with a million fingerprints, a heavily made-up woman I'd place around seventy chews gum. Beyond her, an open door leads into a small apartment decorated with delicate framed furniture.

We show her our badges and introduce ourselves.

She doesn't seem impressed, alarmed, nothing. She simply snaps her gum. "You got a warrant?"

"Why don't we start with your name," I suggest.

"Gilda. You got a warrant?"

"Are you the owner?" Vaughn asks.

"Yes. You got a warrant?"

I hold up the photo of Rebecca and Cathy. "You seen these two?"

Gilda doesn't look at the photo. "Nope."

"Why don't you look again?" I move in closer.

This time she looks. "Nope."

Vaughn shifts, propping his elbow on the counter. "You rent to minors?"

"Nope."

I take the picture back. "What are we going to find if we do get a warrant?"

"Good, hardworking Americans just stopping for some rest on their journeys. 'We'll leave the light on,' and all that." Gilda smirks.

"We hear you offer room and board in exchange for services," I say. "If we talk to that woman in Room 2 giving the truck driver head, are we going to discover she works for you?"

"Sure, I offer a complimentary stay for those less fortunate than I. There's no crime in that."

"Yeah, you're a regular Mother Teresa," Vaughn says.

SEVEN

Monday, 9 p.m.

WE PULL up in front of the station. "By the way, how did your exam go?" I ask as Vaughn gets out.

"Pretty dang good. I'll know the results in a few days."

The glass door to the reception area opens. "Go on now. Git!" Sergeant Rogers manhandles a skinny woman with a backpack nearly as big as her from the station.

"Please," she begs. "I'm not trying to cause any problems. My friend is missing. Why can't I file a report?"

"Yeah, yeah, yeah. All y'all are missing, aren't you? It's why you're living in a gutter." He pushes her. "Go on. Find somewhere to get a bath. You stink."

She stumbles forward, tripping and falling over shoes that are too big for her feet. She glances up at me right as my partner reaches her side. I get a better look at her face. It's the woman from the photo—Rebecca.

I put my vehicle in park and get out. By the time I make

it to their side, Sergeant Rogers has one of her skinny arms and Vaughn the other. She's looking between them, confused.

"This is an A and B conversation," Rogers says to Vaughn. "You can C your way out of it."

"My partner and I need to talk to this woman," Vaughn calmly responds.

"Yeah, well, she needs to get on her way before she causes any more problems."

"What problems is she causing?" Vaughn asks.

"She refused to leave. She threatened to camp out in the lobby until someone took her seriously. It's either tossing her in a cell or moving on. I'm making sure she chooses the latter." He yanks her. "Come on, girl."

Rebecca's eyes widen. She looks at me.

Shit.

I step up. "Sergeant, mind if we talk to her?"

"Yes, I mind!"

Thankfully, Sheriff Owens picks that moment to walk from the station. He comes up short when he sees the four of us. "What's going on?"

"I'll tell ya what's going on!" Rogers yells. "These two underlings are putting their nose where it don't belong."

The sheriff looks right at me.

I say, "Sir, we do need to speak with this woman. It's about Memorial Gardens."

Rebecca gasps. "Did you find Cathy?" Tears flood her eyes. "Is she okay?"

Sergeant Rogers throws his hands up. "Fine." He releases Rebecca and dramatically stomps back into the station.

The sheriff looks between me and my partner. "You got this?"

"Yes," I say. "Thank you."

As he walks away, Vaughn turns to Rebecca. "Ma'am, have you eaten tonight? How about we grab some food and talk?"

EIGHT

Monday, 9:45 p.m.

AFTER SENDING my brother a text to let him know I'm running even later than I thought, we load Rebecca into my SUV. She's silent as I drive to McDonald's.

Now seated outside, Rebecca begins eating her Big Mac.

"Thank you," she says quietly. "I can't remember the last time I ate McDonald's. I used to love it as a kid."

"You're welcome." Smiling, Vaughn dunks a few fries into a vanilla milkshake and eats them.

I'm not hungry, but I select a McNugget, swipe it through mustard, and nibble it.

I let her get several bites in before I ask the first question. "Rebecca, what can you tell us about Cathy?"

Mouth full, she asks, "She's dead, isn't she?"

"What makes you say that?" I reply.

"Why else would you bring me here? How do you know Cathy and me are friends?"

From my back jeans pocket, I slide out the photo I took from the corkboard at Francis House. I place it on the picnic table in front of Rebecca.

She begins to cry. "We've been best friends for a long time. More like sisters. I'm older by ten years. We've been living in this area for months now. She just turned forty. I made her a ring."

"What kind of ring?" Vaughn hands her a napkin.

"Twines of silver with a moonstone in it." She blows her nose. "I gave it to her late yesterday afternoon. We were walking in Memorial Gardens. We were talking about her daughter. Then she cut off into the woods to go to the bathroom. I kept walking down the trail. She never came back out. I looked all over. But soon it became dark and I couldn't see anymore. I spent all day today hitting the usual spots—Tent City, Iris Motel, Francis House...but no one had seen her." Her face turns hard. "Did Twitch have something to do with this?"

"Twitch?" I ask.

"Yeah, we came here with him. He's horrible. I keep trying to ditch him, but Cathy won't let me. I told her he was bad news." Rebecca pushes her food away. "Is there any way you can find her daughter?"

"Find her?"

"Cathy saw her at Francis House. That's all I know. She told me a little bit about her over the years. Something about losing custody. She'd be about twenty now. I guess it was the first time Cathy had seen her since she was a little girl. Took her by surprise, that's for sure." Rebecca looks at the picture again. Her lips wobble.

"Do you know the daughter's name?"

Rebecca shakes her head. "Like I said, Cathy saw her at Francis House. Said she was wearing khakis with a blue top and a white cap." She sniffs. "Oh, she drove away in a van. But there are so many vans that come and go from that place, ya know?"

"What about Cathy's last name?" I ask. "Do you know it?"

"No. Whatever, not like last names are important. She was my best and only friend. That's all that matters." Her breath catches. She wipes her eyes with a napkin.

Reaching over, Vaughn clasps her forearm, offering comfort. Rebecca smiles a little, accepting.

"Can you describe Cathy?" Vaughn asks.

"Average height, like five-five. About like me. Yesterday she was wearing yellow shorts and a white T-shirt. Short hair that's black with a little gray. Heavy. Carries a blue backpack." Rebecca looks between us. "Am I right? Is she dead?"

Gently, my partner says, "There were things done to her body that make identification difficult. Thanks to you though we're getting close. That ring you mentioned? Our person was wearing one just like that. Would you be willing to look at a picture?"

She blows her nose again, before nodding.

On his phone, Vaughn sifts through the many photos taken at the crime scene. He finds one zoomed in on the ring. He shows it to Rebecca. "Is this the one you gave her?"

Sadness creeps into her face, followed slowly by more tears. "Yes, that's the one I gave her."

For several seconds we sit quietly. Rebecca stares at the photo of her and Cathy. Eventually, she turns it over and slides it back to me. She gathers her partially eaten burger and fries and puts them in the paper bag they came in. She tucks it down inside her burgundy backpack. "If you do figure out who her daughter is, will you let me know? I'd like to introduce myself and let her know how great her mom was. Cathy would want her daughter to know she was sorry."

"We'll see what we can do." Vaughn pushes to his feet. "Do you have a place to sleep tonight? If not, I'd like to treat you to a hotel."

"That's kind. Thank you."

WE TAKE REBECCA TO A HOTEL, pay for one night, and leave her to enjoy a hot shower and an actual bed. As we drive away, I roll the windows down, letting in the warm September air. In a couple more weeks the weather will transition into fall.

Tyler said he wants to be an old-fashioned ghost for Halloween. I don't care what he is, I simply love that he still wants to dress up. Maybe I'll do a ghost as well. We'll take two big white sheets, cut holes for eyes, and there you have it—an old-fashioned ghost.

I glance over to my partner, about to ask if he wants to join us in the ghost theme, but he's quietly looking out the passenger side window.

"You okay?" I venture.

"No, I'm not okay." He glances over at me. "That woman, Cathy, has a daughter that may or may not care her mother is dead. Once upon a time, Cathy was young and probably happy and full of big dreams. Then life happened and she spent her dying moments being tortured at the hands of some lunatic who violently stabbed her, burned her, pulled her teeth, and probably robbed her of what little she had in that singed backpack. Her body may not even be claimed. She'll be cremated and disposed of like garbage."

His voice is so full of passion, it robs me of speech.

Shaking his head, he looks back out the window. "You don't get it."

"Get what?"

He doesn't answer me.

Many minutes go by with neither of us talking. Eventually, I pull back into the station and park next to his Mini Cooper. He doesn't get out. I wait.

I've worked with him for five months now. I know his expressions. But when he looks at me across the dark car, his tormented face is one I've never seen before.

In my seat, I shift, making sure I look him directly in the eyes. "I want you to know that you taught me an important lesson today. You showed me how to be empathetic. Thank you."

He doesn't respond to that. He simply keeps staring at me.

Then with a nod, he turns away and gets out. He doesn't look at me as he climbs in his Mini Cooper and drives away.

NINE

I WAKE Tyler and while he's in the shower, I make him an omelet with cheddar, spinach, and tomato. I don't normally make him breakfast unless it's Sunday, but I owe him for being out so late.

He takes exactly one bite before saying, "Work late more often. I like it when you guilty-cook."

"Ha-ha."

He busies himself flipping through a magazine. Idly, I watch him as I eat my toast with avocado. Usually, I wake up thinking of my latest case, but this morning I haven't thought of Cathy, the homeless woman, once. I've been thinking of Rylan Scott on death row.

The folder I found in Grandpa's shed is in my bedroom. I leave Tyler to eat his omelet and carry my plate to my room.

As I finish my toast, I flip through the folder finding the

number I want—the foster home where Rylan's daughter, Mackenzie Scott, was placed ten years ago.

It's early, but I dial anyway. A woman answers. "Hello?"

I hear kids in the background. "Yes, hi. My name is Detective Nell Brach. Are you Mrs. Witherspoon?"

"I am. How can I help you?"

"Ten years ago a young girl was placed with you named Mackenzie Scott. Do you remember her?"

"Of course, I do. Poor thing was so traumatized she could barely communicate. All she did was draw X's. So many X's. Strangest thing. I was beyond relieved when she moved. I was truly scared."

"Scared of what?"

"We were being followed. I told the investigator that, but he dismissed me. Captain Bacote was his name. I figured whoever killed Paige Bell wanted Mackenzie dead, seeing as how she was the only witness."

"Rylan Scott was convicted of that murder."

"Yes," Mrs. Witherspoon says. "But what other explanation is there? Thank God that sheriff stepped in and helped. Brach was his name. Wait a minute, didn't you say that's your name?"

"Yes. Sheriff Brach was my grandfather."

"Well, he was the only one who believed me and that Mackenzie was in danger. To this day I think that little girl would've been killed if he hadn't stepped in and helped. He came and got her in the middle of the night. Told me he'd found a new home for her. That was the last I saw her. Is she okay?"

"I hope so."

We exchange a few more words. I say goodbye, hang up, and move on to tracking down Captain Joe Bacote.

A LONGTIME FRIEND to my grandfather and the lead investigator on the Paige Bell case, Captain Joe Bacote still lives in Knoxville at the same address he did ten years ago. After a quick dive into our state system, I note he retired right after Rylan Scott's conviction.

I send him a brief email requesting a phone call. He responds almost instantly with a suggestion to video chat.

With thick white hair and a matching bushy mustache, he looks exactly like he did at my grandfather's funeral.

In the wide-angle camera, Captain Bacote smiles at me. Behind him, I note a small flat screen mounted to the wall, a tiny kitchenette, and two swivel captain chairs. He's in an RV.

"Nell, how are you? My God, I can't believe you're a detective now. My, how time flies."

"True. I take it you're traveling?"

He motions around the small space. "Meet my new home. We spend more time in this thing than our actual home."

Mrs. Bacote walks into view. Like her husband, the last time I saw her was at the funeral. Her hair was dark then. She's let it go gray, and it hangs in long ringlets pinned back on both sides. She waves. "How ya doing?"

"Fine, Mrs. Bacote. You?"

"Couldn't be any better if you served me a moon pie and an RC Cola."

I laugh.

She kisses her husband on the cheek, grabs her purse, and then steps from the RV to give us privacy.

Captain Bacote waves goodbye before turning back to

me. "My goodness, you look just like your mother did at your age."

That brings a smile to my face.

"Time sure does fly. I should've reached out after the funeral and everything that happened with your mom. But...life, you know."

He's right, he should have reached out. But I keep that to myself and instead just nod.

"Your grandfather was so proud of you. Nell this and Nell that. He thought of you more as a daughter than a grand. I was truly sad when he passed."

I allow a beat to go by, recognizing the sentiment. "I won't take up much of your time," I say. "In my email to you, I mentioned Rylan Scott. I'm not sure if you know this or not but he's requested to see me. He's set to die by lethal injection at the end of the week."

"Yes, I plan on being there."

I wasn't expecting him to say that.

Would I want to watch someone die? Maybe. It depends on the circumstances. If Tyler had perished at the hands of his kidnapper, yes, I would want justice. And I would want to see it carried out. Given I killed him, that's a moot point.

"My grandfather believed he was innocent. Are you able to shed light on that?"

"I wish I would've never asked him to consult on the case. But he had just wrapped on something else and was receiving a lot of media attention. I got pressure from the higher-ups to invite him onto the team. Plus, it looks good when our neighboring counties work together. Frankly, though, he stuck his nose where it didn't belong. He went over my head and pulled strings. To this day I don't know where that little girl is. She was our only witness."

"I understand she wasn't a reliable one."

"True. She was in shock. But with the help of a child psychiatrist, we hoped that would turn around. Of course that never transpired."

"Why were you convinced he was guilty?"

"No forced entry. Ry—"

"That doesn't mean anything. Hell, half the time I don't lock my front door."

Captain Bacote holds up a hand. "Let me finish. No forced entry. Wearing gloves, Rylan walked right in the front door like he had done so many times before. He thought he was killing his wife when instead he stabbed the twin. After the murder, he fled through the kitchen window which overlooked an alley. He was panicked and covered in blood. He stashed the weapon in his truck. Hours went by. His conscience got the best of him. He'd killed the wrong woman. He returned and called nine-one-one. His prints may not have been on the murder weapon or the window he went out of but they were all over the apartment, Paige's body, and the area around her."

"It was his apartment, correct? My home has my fingerprints everywhere."

The captain just looks at me.

"Where did he think his daughter was?" I ask.

"The neighbor's place. She often watched the little girl. The neighbor told us that Paige had picked the girl up earlier in the day when she realized her sister was on a bender."

"If Rylan's conscience got the best of him, as you say, then he admitted to things?"

"Eventually, yes. At first, though, he maintained the same story. He was at work, came home, and found Paige on the floor. He tried to revive her, to no avail. That's when he called for help."

Sounds plausible. "If he was at work, then he had an alibi," I state the obvious.

"No. His truck was parked right outside the apartment the whole time. Several people saw it there. Rylan claims it wouldn't start. He caught a ride to the job site. He was an under-the-table day worker. Here one day, there the next. The construction site where he claimed to be that day failed to corroborate his alibi."

"Because they didn't want to get busted for under-the-table workers."

Captain Bacote sighs. "You sound like your grandfather."

"You said 'eventually, yes.' Did he change his story because he was afraid for his daughter's life? He took the fall to get the attention off of her?"

"Again, so much like your grandfather. Why does anyone change their plea? He knew he was guilty."

No, I don't buy it. "Why was Grandpa so sure of Rylan's innocence?"

"No prints on the weapon, though as I said it *was* found in Rylan's truck *and* covered in Paige Bell's blood. But your grandfather had a 'gut' feeling about Rylan. They spoke several times. 'I know a killer's eyes, and Rylan doesn't have them.' He spent a lot of energy looking into Rylan's wife. He was convinced she had pissed someone off and they'd finally had enough. That's why she took off and abandoned her daughter because she knew that stabbing was meant for her. Then there was the thing with the foster mom claiming the little girl was being followed."

"You didn't believe that?"

"I think your grandfather was an alarmist. He freaked

the foster mother out. He called her every day to make sure all was okay. Paranoia grows fast when someone is there feeding into it."

I agree, but my grandfather was not an alarmist. Many other things, sure, but not that.

We grow silent after that.

Captain Bacote gives me the space to work through things.

I think of the file I found in the shed and of my grandfather's notes. The crayon X's come to mind, as does the word "tattoo." The captain didn't mention either one. The girl's new name was redacted, as was her new address. For now, I don't bring any of that up. I'm not sure if Captain Bacote knows any more than what he told me. And if my grandfather felt that it was necessary to protect that little girl, the only witness, then there is a reason.

Captain Bacote leans forward, getting closer to the camera. "I'll tell you this. If it would have gone to trial, that jury would have found Rylan Scott guilty. That's how airtight the evidence was. And one more thing. Rylan Scott has a history of attacking prison guards, other inmates, and even the chaplain. Those aren't actions of an innocent man."

No, they're the actions of a desperate one.

"Listen, I've got to go," the captain says. "But you tell Sergeant Rogers I said hello."

"Excuse me?"

"He used to be one of mine. Good man. I gave him a stellar reference when he said he was moving over to your area."

TEN

Tuesday, 10 a.m.

AT THE STATION, I find Lisbeth, our new IT tech, in her cubicle. Right out of college and beyond intelligent, we are lucky to have her. I expect she'll move on once she gets some experience here.

"Hey, Lisbeth." I step up beside her.

With an adorable pixie cut, giant brown eyes, and flawless dark skin, I think of a porcelain doll every time I look at her.

"Hey, Nell." She grins. "What's up?"

I hand her the photo of nine-year-old Mackenzie Scott, followed by the redacted page. "This has nothing to do with my current homeless woman murder case, but I'd still like you to move it to the top of your to-do list. It's connected to the Rylan Scott execution this coming Friday. I want to keep this between you and me, okay?"

"Absolutely." She looks at the picture of the devastated

little girl taken a day after Paige Bell's murder. Lisbeth's smile fades. "She looks terrified."

"Ten years ago she witnessed the murder of her aunt, Paige Bell. Her father is Rylan Scott. Her name then was Mackenzie Scott. It's since been changed. She used to live in Knoxville. Any chance you can figure out her new name? That redacted page is all I have."

"Possibly." She taps the photo. "I can also age this if you want, so you can see what she looks like now."

"Perfect."

"But I can't make any promises on the redacted stuff."

"Do what you can."

Leaving her to it, I find Vaughn in the break room. Today he wears a gray tie with black mustaches all over it. Busy making his daily green tea, I pour coffee, adding coconut milk.

"I stopped by Francis House this morning," he says, "following up with Rebecca's mention of Cathy seeing her daughter there. Preacher Mitch said that Cathy had already asked him the same thing. He doesn't know. They have loads of volunteers coming and going, all ages. Could be anybody." Vaughn blows on his tea before sipping. "Then as I was leaving, I saw a young woman get into a van with *Larson Cleaning* on the side. Get this, she was wearing khaki pants and a blue shirt but no white cap. I did a little digging. Larson Cleaning is a small family business based in Iris. The tag on the van is registered to Destiny Larson."

On his phone, he pulls up a photo of her license. She's got shoulder-length bleached hair, tan skin, a pierced nose, and wears bright blue eye shadow with fake lashes. If this is Cathy's daughter, I'm not seeing it. I note her birthday. She just turned twenty.

Vaughn continues, "Might be her, might not. It's something though."

"Let's pay her a visit. Also, let's not forget the Twitch fellow they arrived with."

My partner nods. "Destiny first."

ELEVEN

Tuesday, 11:30 a.m.

DESTINY LARSON'S neighborhood reminds me of mine —small old homes with equally small yards. I pull in behind the van that Vaughn saw leaving Francis House.

Tiny green bushes with purple blooms line the brick walkway leading up to the porch. Three wooden steps take us up to the front door.

Vaughn follows, coming to stand beside me.

A pale yellow door is closed. I don't see a bell, so I knock.

Inside, footsteps stir. The door opens. Holding a half-sandwich and chewing, Destiny Larson glances between us. She looks exactly like she did on her driver's license— bleached hair, fake lashes, blue eye shadow, and nose piercing. She wears khaki pants with a blue polo that has *Larson Cleaning* embroidered over the left breast.

Now that I'm right here in front of her, I try again to see

the similarity between her and Cathy. Unfortunately, it's not there.

We show our badges.

"Destiny Larson?" Vaughn asks.

She stops chewing, glancing at my partner's tie, before looking back up. "Yes?"

Before I left the station, I scanned the photo that I took from the corkboard at Francis House. I cropped out Rebecca, leaving us with a zoomed-in picture of Cathy only. I show it to Destiny. "Do you know this woman?"

She leans in, looking at it. She shakes her head.

"This woman is not your mother?" I ask.

"*What?*" She snatches the photo from me. She studies it, and studies it, and continues studying it for so long that I'm sure she's going to positively identify the homeless woman. Instead, Destiny hands it back. "No. That's not her."

"How do you know?"

She disappears and comes back carrying a framed black-and-white photo of a beautiful woman wearing a scarf tied around her head and holding a baby. "Sorry about that. You took me off guard. *This* was my mother. She died not long after this picture was taken. I was raised by my grammy."

"And your father?"

Destiny shrugs. "Never knew him."

Vaughn glances past her into an empty home. "Is your grammy home?"

"No." Sadness creeps into her expression. "She passed away last year."

"I'm sorry for your loss," I say.

"Thank you."

Vaughn hands her a card. "Hold onto that in case you ever need anything."

She takes the card, says goodbye, and closes the door.

Back in my SUV, Vaughn says, "She looked at that picture a little too long."

"Agreed. But, I get it. We took her off guard. She's not our girl, though."

"Maybe, maybe not. Play things out. Cathy gets pregnant, has little Destiny, and decides she doesn't want to be a mommy. She hits the road, leaving Grammy to raise the baby. Grammy decides it's easier to tell Destiny her deadbeat mother is dead. Then she gives her that photo to remember her by."

"And if the mother returned?"

"Good point. I guess Grammy was gambling that wouldn't happen."

"Nah, Destiny's not our girl. Did you see the woman with the scarf tied around her head? That was definitely not a young Cathy."

Vaughn studies the photo I took from the corkboard. "I don't know, twenty years ago, she was probably a looker. Put a scarf around her head and makeup on her... Or maybe Grammy bought a picture at Target and told Destiny it was her mother."

I laugh. "Drop it."

His stomach growls. "You hungry?"

"I can eat."

We're a few miles down the road looking for a place to grab a bite when I get a text over Bluetooth.

Lisbeth: Check your inbox.

"What's in your inbox?" Vaughn asks.

"Information about Rylan Scott's daughter, Mackenzie." I fill Vaughn in on the file I found in the shed, the call I had with the foster mother, followed by the video chat with

Captain Bacote.

"You do realize it's not an active case," my partner says. "Rylan Scott is being executed at the end of this week for a crime he admitted to doing."

"There are too many holes for me to ignore. Don't worry, I won't let it infringe on our investigation into Cathy's murder. Plus, Rylan Scott did request to see me."

"You going?"

"I am. Sooner rather than later, for obvious reasons." I hang a right into a convenience store. We each grab something to go.

As we sit in my SUV eating, I bring up the email from Lisbeth. Attached is the aged photo of Mackenzie Scott. I nearly choke on my granola bar. "Holy shit." I show it to Vaughn as I dial Lisbeth back.

"What's up?" she says.

"Can you put bleached hair on the aged Mackenzie, fake lashes, a nose ring, and blue eye shadow?"

"That's specific."

"Now."

"Hang tight." Her mouse clicking echoes over Bluetooth. "Okay, just sent it."

The new photo loads. I thank Lisbeth and I hang up.

Dumbfounded, my partner and I stare.

"Mackenzie Scott and Destiny Larson are the same person," he says.

"Which means *if* Cathy is her mother, that makes our homeless woman Natalie Scott." Wife of Rylan and twin sister to Paige Bell.

TWELVE

Tuesday, 3:15 p.m.

LEAVING my partner to handle things, I drive into Knoxville to visit Rylan Scott.

I sit in a private room with no cameras. Dressed in a white jumpsuit, Rylan Scott is escorted in by two guards. He's chained to eyebolts on both the floor and the anchored table between us. The two guards leave.

He breathes out, staring at me through light blue eyes. Destiny has his eyes.

"Thank you for coming," he says.

I nod.

On the table next to my left hand is the folder from the shed. I've yet to determine if I'm going to open it. "I heard just yesterday that you requested to see me. Otherwise, I would've been here sooner."

"I figured."

"How can I help you, Mr. Scott?"

"If I wrote a letter to my daughter would you give it to her?"

"What makes you think I know where your daughter is?"

"I'm not sure you do, but your grandfather knew. With him being gone, you're my only shot."

Sliding the file over, I place my hands on top. He glances down, then back up.

"I've thoroughly reviewed your information. I spoke with your daughter's foster mom from ten years ago. I also chatted with the investigative officer. I'd like to hear everything from your mouth."

"Why? I'm guilty. I stabbed my sister-in-law, Paige Bell."

"You pled guilty only after you heard about your daughter, the only witness, being followed. It's just you and me here. Tell me the truth, please."

"I don't know why it matters," he mumbles.

"It matters to me."

Rylan looks down at his chained hands. He picks a hangnail. "I knew Cathy was up to no good."

"Cathy?"

"Natalie Catherine Scott, my wife. Paige had grown up calling her Cathy, so I did as well. Pretty much everyone else knew her as Natalie." He lifts his gaze back to mine. "She was suddenly flush with money. I didn't know how she was getting it and she wouldn't tell me. I figured she was mixed up with the wrong crowd. That kind of stuff only lasts for so long. When I found Paige on that kitchen floor, for one brief second I thought it was Cathy, and I wasn't surprised. *You pissed off the wrong person*, I thought. But then I realized it was Paige. Immediately, I dialed emergency. I tried stopping the blood. There was so much of it. I tried CPR, though I didn't know what I was doing. Hell, I didn't even know she was already dead. I sure as hell didn't know Mackenzie was in the bathroom watching the whole thing.

"The cops showed up, then EMT. Before I knew it, I was being handcuffed. My daughter was taken into custody. And my wife was nowhere to be found. A few weeks later Sheriff Brach came to me, told me about Mackenzie being followed, and suggested I plead guilty. I didn't hesitate. It was clear whoever killed Paige thought he was killing Cathy. With my daughter the only witness, she was in the crosshairs. I asked the sheriff if he could protect Mackenzie. He said he would make sure she remained unseen. Weeks after that he visited me. Told me he'd given my daughter a new identity and a new home. Told me she was safe.

"The first few years he would visit me and show me pictures of Mackenzie. I looked so forward to that. But then he passed and the pictures stopped." Rylan brightens. "Do you have one?"

"Let me see what I can do about that." My fingers tap the folder. "Anything else about your wife that you can think of? What did she do for a living? I don't have a clear picture of that."

"She was a stripper. Wild and free. We met at the club where she worked. She gave me a lap dance. I was there for a bachelor party. There was something different about her. I fell hard. We married on a whim. Eloped to Vegas. It was only after we got back that I discovered the real her. She tended toward violence, drugs, and alcohol. More than once she punched me. I never punched back. I took it, though. So many times I found her passed out in the bushes leading up to our apartment. I also frequently found her in bed with other men, and women. She stopped partying when she found out she was pregnant. I'll give her that much. Truth is, I stayed for my daughter. I knew if I left, I'd probably never get to see her again." He gives a dejected chuckle. "What does it matter? Look where I am?"

His gaze moves past my shoulder. "Cold Steel six-inch tactical folding knife," he mutters. "I didn't know what that was. I do now. They found it in my truck, parked right there at the curb. It was covered in Paige's blood."

"Can you fill in a gap for me?"

"I don't want you to prove my innocence, if that's what you're hoping. I'm giving my life for my daughter."

"No ulterior motive. Just a gap." Opening the folder, I slide out the bold crayon X's. "Any idea what this is?"

"Mackenzie kept drawing that over and over again. I don't know what it is. Sorry."

I put the drawing back.

"Detective Brach, do you have any idea what happened to my wife? She signed over rights to our daughter and disappeared. That was ten years ago. Any idea at all?"

"Let me double-check a couple of things before I answer that question." For one long moment, I look directly into his eyes, trying to connect with my gut instinct. I don't necessarily see innocence, but I do see resignation. And fear. "Mr. Scott, I want you to know that I have listened and I have heard you. If you write that letter, I will do everything in my power to get it to your daughter."

"But will you do everything in your power to continue making sure she's unseen?"

THIRTEEN

Tuesday, 5:45 p.m.

ON THE WAY back to White Quail from Knoxville, I dial Vaughn.

He says, "I had Lisbeth do her aging magic on a ten-year-old photo of Natalie Scott. Cut her hair, put gray in it, and add about fifty pounds and it's a match to Cathy."

"Rylan called her Cathy while we were talking. Still, we're going to need DNA."

"Already requested a match to the sister, Paige Bell."

"Perfect."

"How did it go with Rylan?" he asks.

"His only request was for me to deliver a letter to his daughter."

"Wow."

"He's not looking for any last-ditch effort to overturn his sentence. He's willingly dying to protect his little girl from the real killer. A lot more was said. Too much to talk about on the phone."

Vaughn says, "Forensics came back. Based on the wounds, a six-inch blade was used."

"Paige was done with a Cold Steel six-inch tactical folding knife. Knives are like guns. Once you find your favorite, you stick with it."

"Tactical, as in former military?"

"Possibly." Or a cop...

"Are you saying the same person did both?" Vaughn asks.

"Same vicious stabbing. Six-inch blade. Ten years later and they finally got the right twin, who, according to Rylan Scott, apparently had gotten mixed up with the wrong crowd and was suddenly rolling in the dough."

"Why wait ten years?"

I say, "Cathy's been living off the grid. Could've taken that long to find her. The killer scraped her identity so we wouldn't make connections."

"The violence behind the kill leans toward a personal vendetta."

"My grandfather was digging into Cathy's past. We need to pick up where he left off." Because if I can prove the same person killed both Paige and Cathy, I'll be able to get a stay of execution. We can put the real killer away. Destiny will remain safe.

"Motivation rooted so deeply that someone waited ten years. That's some vendetta."

I ask, "Do you think forensics can match Paige's stab marks to Cathy's?"

I can't see him, but I can feel him smile. "I already asked. The answer is no. Forensics can't use pictures. They would need Paige's body."

That's not going to happen.

I spy my exit up ahead and click on my blinker. "Other than Lisbeth, you haven't told anyone anything, correct?"

"Correct."

"I'm going to swing by the station and get everything from Lisbeth to put back in my grandfather's file. Can you come by my house tonight?" I steer my SUV down the off-ramp. "I want to dive into Cathy's past. I also want to research the woman who raised Destiny. And we still have Twitch to figure out." I hear Vaughn's blinker turn on. "Where are you?" I ask.

"I'm leaving Destiny's neighborhood. I wanted to get eyes on her. Make sure she's okay. If someone figured out who Cathy was, they may already know who Destiny is."

Not likely, is my first thought. But he does have a point. "Rebecca did say that Cathy told everyone she saw her daughter."

"It'll send up red flags if we suddenly take her into protective custody."

"Agreed."

"We don't even know if Destiny remembers who she really is."

"She was nine when she witnessed the murder. Trauma like that burrows in deep. Add into that the lie Grammy told her about her mother dying, and you're right—she may honestly think she is Destiny Larson."

FOURTEEN

Tuesday, 8 p.m.

HEADLIGHTS FLASH across my living room window. I peek out, not recognizing Vaughn's Mini Cooper. Instead, a maroon SUV pulls in with a Lyft sticker on the windshield. Vaughn sits passenger side, not in the back. The woman behind the wheel sees me, giving me a timid wave.

That's Charlotte Swift. Because of her, we were able to solve the murder of a thirteen-year-old girl. The last time I saw Charlotte, I wasn't exactly nice. Now, though, I wave back, letting her know I'm not a bitch. I was just stressed.

Vaughn and Charlotte exchange a kiss, he climbs out, then she pulls away.

I open my front door. "You and Charlotte Swift, huh?"

"Yes." He grins.

"How long has that been going on?"

"It's brand-new."

"Tell me *all* about it," I say like we're girlfriends and not partners in crime.

He laughs as he follows me into the house. "Nothing really to tell. I was in Target a couple of months ago. I saw her looking at pet supplies. We struck up a conversation. Then I saw her again at a red light. We were stopped right beside each other. Anyway, fast-forward and we've had several dates. We just got a bite to eat."

I study his face. "You look happy."

"I am." He looks around. "Where's Little Man?"

"In his room. You can go say hi. Meet me at the kitchen table."

Minutes later we're seated beside each other. The contents of my grandfather's file are strewn across the table. Vaughn sifts through it, studying the redacted page, the drawing with the bold X's, the detailed notes, the photos... From Cathy's file, he takes out the pictures of her stabbed body and places them next to the ones of her twin sister. Seeing them side by side like this is eye-opening.

I say, "Rylan doesn't want a stay of execution, but I can do this. *We* can do this. We'll have the DNA test by tomorrow night that proves our homeless woman and Paige Bell are twin sisters. Both murders were done with a six-inch blade. If we can find the murder weapon used on Cathy, I would bet it's a tactical folding knife just like what was used on Paige. That leaves us with Destiny-slash-Mackenize. Assuming she's blocked the event from her mind, if we can get her to remember the details, *anything*, we have a shot at filing for a stay." I hold up the drawing paper with the X's on it. "If we can get her to tell us what this is."

Vaughn runs a hand over his slicked-back hair. "I've been thinking about the word 'vendetta.' It's no coincidence Cathy was murdered the same week her husband is set to die. It's poetic justice. Like the killer's been waiting for this week to arrive."

"Interesting take."

"And even more reason to carefully monitor Destiny. Yes, she was the only witness. She is the one person who can identify the real killer. More importantly, she is Rylan and Cathy's daughter."

"As in the killer would target her no matter if she was a witness or not?"

"Maybe..."

"Sounds like a lot of patience and planning." I sit back, looking at it from that angle. "Doesn't the violence of the kill seem more spur of the moment? The words 'patience' and 'planning' don't match the viciousness of the stabbing. At least in my mind, they don't."

"Just throwing ideas out, seeing what sticks."

"Of course. Likewise." From under a pile of pictures that I found in an old album, I pull out a black-and-white photo of my grandparents with a pretty, dark-haired woman. "While I was waiting on you, I did some digging into the lady who raised Destiny Larson. She was a long-time friend of my grandparents. They all went to high school together. She never married and never had children. She used to babysit my mother. She had a small cleaning business her whole life. She used to live here in White Quail. When she adopted Destiny, they moved one town over. She was the perfect person to raise, and hide, one scared little girl."

"Hide in plain sight."

I pick up the photo of Cathy that was taken ten years ago. Once upon a time, she was a beautiful woman. That picture Destiny showed us of her as a baby with her mother is definitely Cathy. I see it now. "What did you do?" I murmur. "Who did you piss off?"

On the table next to everything else sits my laptop. Vaughn turns it around. "Let's see if we can figure that out."

FIFTEEN

Wednesday, 8 a.m.

I KNOCK on Destiny's door. It takes her a full minute to answer. Dressed ready for work in her khaki pants and navy monogrammed polo, she smiles. "Oh, hi. You again."

"Good morning." I show her the black-and-white photo that I found. "Our grandparents knew each other."

"No way." She takes the picture, giving it a long study. "Wow, my grammy was beautiful."

"Yes, she was. You can keep that if you want."

"Really? Cool."

Next, I hand her my card. "My partner gave you his, but I wanted to make sure you have mine as well."

"Okay." She takes it, but the gesture seems to confuse her.

"One question and then I'll let you get to work."

She nods.

"Do you know the names Rylan, Natalie, and Mackenzie Scott?" Closely, I watch her face, looking for any hint of anything—that she knows who she really is; that she has no clue; that she's scared; that she's cautious; that she's forming a lie to tell.

"No, I don't think so," she finally says.

I nod. "That was my only question. Keep my card handy."

"Will do."

Back in the SUV, I text Vaughn:

Me: Destiny doesn't know she's Mackenzie Scott.

Vaughn: With last night's search on Natalie Scott giving us what we already knew—that she was a stripper—we're left with Rebecca. Other than Rylan Scott, she's known her the longest. Maybe Cathy said something to her about her past and how she was suddenly rolling in the dough.

Me: Plus, Twitch is still dangling out there.

Vaughn: Agreed. See you in a few.

SIXTEEN

Wednesday, 8:45 a.m.

WHEN I PULL into the station, Vaughn is waiting in the parking lot. He climbs in. "I just got off the phone with Preacher Mitch. He said he overheard some of his patrons this morning talking about Rebecca. Apparently, she got beat up pretty badly. Someone saw her under the overpass near the Iris Motel. The preacher was planning on checking on her. I said we would."

FIFTEEN MINUTES LATER, we see her huddled under the bridge up against the embankment surrounded by over-grown grass and random litter.

She's not moving.

My gut knots.

Vaughn is out of the vehicle before I even stop it. "Rebecca, can you hear me?"

She doesn't respond.

I cut the engine and jump out.

Cautiously, he climbs the embankment to where she is. I follow. Her backpack is on her shoulders. As I draw near, I notice the lumps and bruises on her face. There's no telling what the rest of her body looks like.

Vaughn squats down. He leans in, about to check for a pulse when her eyes flutter open.

She shrinks back. "No," she groans. "Please."

"It's me, Detective London, and right here is Detective Brach. You're okay. We won't hurt you."

"Leave me alone."

"Who did this to you?" I squat down next to my partner.

She shakes her head.

"Let us take you to a clinic." Vaughn reaches for her.

"I'm fine." She pushes away. "Please, leave me alone. I can't be seen talking to you."

"Who told you that?" I ask.

She struggles to stand and we help her. When she's on her feet, she staggers in place. I'm afraid she's going to fall down the embankment. Gently, I grasp her arm. She winces.

"You may have broken something," I say.

"I didn't break anything." She pulls from my grasp. "I'm just beaten up. I've had worse." Sniffing, she dabs at the blood seeping from a cut on her bottom lip.

She walks down the grassy slope with us huddling beside her in case she falls.

Vaughn's voice comes quiet, nearly deadly. "Who did this to you?"

"Twitch, okay? Now leave me alone." When we reach the pavement, she walks away.

We have no choice but to let her go.

SEVENTEEN

Wednesday, 10:30 a.m.

AT FRANCIS HOUSE, we touch base with Preacher Mitch. "Please tell me you found Rebecca," he says.

"We did," I confirm. "But she walked off. We're looking for Twitch. What can you tell us about him?"

"Supposedly he's retired Special Ops." Preacher Mitch takes a photo off his corkboard and hands it to me. "He's bad news."

With a buzzed head and a bushy beard, he's a squirrelly-looking man.

Vaughn glances at the photo I'm holding. "What's your definition of bad news?"

"He steals other people's food. He makes women do things to him. He's got a foul mouth. And he refuses to put away his knives. He's always showing them off. He's got quite the collection."

"You said that Cathy and Rebecca arrived here with

him. Do you know how long they've been traveling together?" Vaughn asks.

The preacher shrugs. "Years, I think. That's normal though. Groups come and go all the time, some stay together, some split off, a couple will settle here, a couple more out at Tent City, some will move on, some will stay... It's different every time."

"If Cathy had a secret, who would she tell it to?" Vaughn asks.

Preacher Mitch laughs. "Everyone. Cathy kind of had a big mouth."

"Where can we find this Twitch?"

EIGHTEEN

Wednesday, 11:30 a.m.

THE HOMELESS ENCAMPMENT, Tent City, has been squatting on abandoned farmland for a couple of years now. We've notified the owner who lives out of the country and doesn't seem to care. As long as they don't cause problems, Sheriff Owens says to leave them be.

Vaughn and I weave through the makeshift tents asking about Twitch. One man hunches over a camping stove stirring a can of soup. He barely looks at the photo we show him as he shakes his head. A woman under a tarp playing solitaire responds the same way. A man curled under a tree napping mutters *No*. A woman sitting cross-legged with a cat in her lap gives a slight nod to the right.

We follow her signal down to the end. With an unkempt gray beard that extends down his neck, a wiry man sits on a bucket. Covered in tattoos and dressed in a white "wife beater" shirt, he sharpens a large military knife with a stone.

He watches us as we approach.

We come to a stop a few feet in front of him.

"Can I help you?" He sucks his teeth.

We show him our badges.

"Put the knife down. Now," I command.

"Make me," he sneers.

I lunge, popping him in the nose with the heel of my hand. The knife flies. He tumbles from the bucket. Roughly I grab him, flip him, and jam his face down into the grass. I grind my knee into his bony spinal cord and cuff him.

Then I yank him to his feet and shove him forward. "Walk."

A string of curses erupts from Twitch's mouth.

I look over to Vaughn, who stands with the knife already bagged, staring at me, smiling.

I shrug. "He said 'make me.'"

NINETEEN

Wednesday, 4 p.m.

TWITCH NOW SITS in an interrogation room. I stand next to Vaughn looking at our suspect through the two-way mirror. In the room with us are his belongings amounting to one military-issued duffel full of clothes, miscellaneous items, and several knives—including a Cold Steel six-inch tactical folding one.

Vaughn references the file he printed after scanning Twitch's prints. "Real name is David Archer. Barely four years in the military. Not special forces. Dishonorably discharged. Forty years old. Last known address is in Knoxville. Has a long list of arrests for drunk and disorderly, trespassing, harassment, domestic violence, etcetera. Ready for this? He has an ex-wife. They were married for less than a year. Million dollars if you guess who."

"Natalie Catherine Scott."

"Married at eighteen. Divorced at nineteen. He joined

the military. And she hooked up with Rylan Scott. Had Destiny at twenty-one. Took off nine years later."

"Cold Steel six-inch tactical folding knife right in his things. How handy." I check my phone to see if we have forensics back on the knife. We don't. "I've got Lisbeth working on where this guy was ten years ago, the day Paige Bell was murdered."

"Okay, say he did Paige and framed Rylan. Why wait this long to do the correct twin? He's been traveling with Cathy and Rebecca. He could've done it any time. He doesn't exactly scream 'patience' and 'planning.'"

"No, but he does scream violent stabbing. Maybe things have been okay between them. Then Cathy did something to piss him off and his rage flared. He tracked her to Memorial Gardens and finally did what he wanted to do all those years ago."

The door opens. Sergeant Rogers steps in. He looks at Twitch through the two-way. "Well, if it isn't ole Twitch. I didn't know he was in this neck of the woods."

Does this man not have anything else to do but interfere with our work?

Vaughn closes the file. "How do you know him?"

"Frequent flyer at my last posting. I busted up quite a few brawls he got in with his girlfriend of the month. Last one he did a number on her. But she refused to file charges, so—" Rogers waves his hand toward the mirror. "Guess he's our problem now. Want me to talk to him?"

"No." I take the file from Vaughn's fingers. "Let's go."

Rogers holds up his hands. "Fine. Don't get your panties in a wad."

My jaw tightens.

I open the door to Twitch's room, fully aware Sergeant Rogers is still over there watching. Vaughn turns on the camera. I sit down across from the man. The dried blood under his nose and beginning bruise give me a tiny bit of satisfaction.

I place my phone face up so I can see when forensics comes in on the knife.

Opening the folder, I show him the photo of Rebecca and Cathy that I took from the corkboard at Francis House. I point to Cathy. "Do you know this woman?"

He leans in. "I sure do. She gives good head."

Vaughn crosses behind him, roughly knocking into his chair. "Sorry about that."

Twitch sneers.

"How long have you been traveling with the two of them?"

"On and off for years."

"What brought you to this area?" I ask.

"Time for me to move on from my cunt of an ex."

Vaughn paces behind him again, jabbing his elbow into his shoulder blade. "Sorry about that."

Twitch glares. "That bitch Rebecca squealed, didn't she? You all think I knifed Cathy? You don't know shit."

"Enlighten us."

He grabs his crotch. "Enlighten this."

Under the table, I kick his kneecap. Hard. He screams.

"Sorry about that," I say.

He snarls. "Whatever. Me and Cathy, we go way back. Hell, she was fucking me the whole time she was with that reject she married."

My phone lights up. I check the message.

Twitch jabs a finger in his chest. "I'm the one she came to when things went to shit. Not that lesbo, Rebecca. Hell, I'm the one Nat—*Cathy* was partying with when—"

"When?"

He pauses. He sits back. He folds his arms. "Maybe I should have a lawyer."

"Maybe." I stand up, showing him my phone. "Because I just got confirmation that the Cold Steel six-inch tactical folding knife we took from you is the murder weapon. And boy is it covered in your prints."

"I didn't do anything! I found that knife in my things. I swear!"

Out in the workroom, Lisbeth flags me down. She hands me a piece of paper. "Credit card receipts from ten years ago put David "Twitch" Archer in Williamsburg, Kentucky, not Knoxville, Tennessee. Note that Natalie Scott signed a couple of them."

Well, crap.

I scan the multiple receipts seeing one from a motel, another from a store where they bought shitloads of beer, another with cartons of cigarettes, and another from a fast-food place. Two of them do have Natalie Scott's signature. I show Vaughn. "Looks like we figured out who Natalie-slash-Cathy was on her bender with when her twin sister was stabbed to death."

"We may not have him for Paige, but we have him for Cathy."

This should excite me, but it doesn't. I wanted him for both.

TWENTY

Wednesday, 6:15 p.m.

AT THE STATION, Twitch's lawyer arrives. We put them in a private room. They've been in there thirty minutes.

Arms folded, I stand at my desk staring at them through the blinds. I want to dig into Cathy's past, and now knowing they were married, Twitch might be the key. He knew her before Rylan did. And according to Twitch, he was "fucking" her the whole time. "We really need that DNA back on Paige and Cathy."

"Nell." Vaughn nudges me, nodding toward the wall-mounted flat screen.

Front and center in our local evening news is Gilda, the Iris Motel owner. She stands at the gate that leads into Memorial Gardens.

Dressed in a long blue vintage skirt, pink ruffled silk blouse, pearls, a white pillbox hat pinned to her poofy brown hair, and makeup so thick you could scrape it off, she looks like a 1950's housewife who became Amish and then a washed-up porn star.

She says, "Our so-called law enforcement spends their days picking on the homeless and people like me who are small business owners. Right here behind me a poor homeless woman was found violently stabbed to death. The most horrendous of murders. And what do the cops do? They harass the other homeless people in the area and arrested one of them earlier today. Just because you're homeless, doesn't mean you're a deviant!"

She straightens up. Hell, she even clutches a bible.

"I'm telling you the man they arrested is a decorated soldier. We should be honoring him, not persecuting him. They didn't even ask him for an alibi. Well, I'm telling you right now, *I'm* his alibi." She punctuates "I'm" with a finger jabbed into the air.

"And I am the one who found the knife that the cops think is their 'smoking gun.' I found it in the dumpster at my motel. If it's the murder weapon, the cops should be looking for whoever dumped it. Because I gave it to the man they're holding *after* the murder occurred.

"Join me now, good citizens, in picketing for his release." Then she salutes, wrongly, I might add, like she's about to go into battle.

The camera moves off of Gilda as the reporter appears. "There you have it, folks. That was—"

"That idiot just gave us a reason to get a warrant." I send Lisbeth a text:

Me: Get me everything you can on the owner of the Iris Motel.

TWENTY-ONE

Wednesday, 8:05 p.m.

AT THE IRIS MOTEL, I slap a warrant onto the counter. Still dressed in her ridiculous outfit, Gilda purses her creamy pink lips, looking at it.

She dramatically waves her arm around the place. "All yours."

Behind us, our team begins the search of the small motel. I knew when we pulled up that she'd scrubbed the place and cleared it of its questionable renters. With an empty parking lot, all the doors open to the rooms, clean windows, the thick curtains pulled back, and a power-washed exterior, we won't find a thing.

Even her office has been scrubbed and has a damn Zen fountain trickling in the corner.

"Let's start with the knife," Vaughn says. "Where did you find it?"

"Out back. Two nights ago. Some raccoons were digging through my garbage cans. I chased them off, and as I was cleaning up the mess they made, I found the knife. It was clean and in perfect condition. I gave it to Twitch because I know how much he likes knives."

"Okay, let's say that's true." I lean against the counter, all casual. "Why then would you give it to a homeless man named Twitch?"

She smiles sickly sweet like she was waiting for that question. "Because he's my son. I'm the reason why he came here from Knoxville. We've been at odds for years. We've recently reconnected. I told him I'd pay him to keep up the place for me. Even told him to stay in one of the rooms, but he likes Tent City better."

Okay, I was not expecting that answer.

"Apple doesn't fall far," Vaughn mutters.

Gilda sneers.

"And you can prove you two were together on Sunday?" I ask.

"I sure can. He was right here, helping me all afternoon. As a thank-you, I took him up the road to the truck stop for blueberry pancakes. It's his favorite." She produces a receipt. "Tons of people saw us eating. We even played pinball while we were there. Then we came back here. I offered to drive him out to Tent City but he opted to stay over here."

"With or without that receipt, know that we will question everyone at that truck stop," Vaughn says.

With a pointy pink nail, she picks the space between her two front teeth. "Anything else?"

VAUGHN and I stand side by side in the station's lobby watching David "Twitch" Archer strut out the door, carrying his belongings. I stare at his back, halfway expecting him to flip us off but he doesn't. He simply walks across the parking lot and gets into a car that Gilda's driving.

"Well, at least we have the murder weapon," my partner says.

Sergeant Rogers comes through the security door that leads into the back. "Was that Twitch I just saw leave?" He hoots. "He's a slippery motherfucker." He slaps Vaughn on the back. "You won't make sergeant this way. Arresting and letting people go?" He tsks. "Take it from someone with twenty-five years, you've gotta be sure before you haul in a fella like Twitch."

"What do you want?" I ask, turning fully to face him.

"Excuse me?"

"You are everywhere we are. Don't you have a job that doesn't involve side comments about me and my partner? It's late. Don't you have a home to go to?"

I expect him to come back at me, but instead, Sergeant Rogers smiles. "Everyone around here knows your Owens' favorite. Eventually, that'll catch up to you. Be careful who you mouth off to." Then with a wink to me, Rogers walks out of the lobby.

"God, I hate him," I say.

"Ditto."

TWENTY-TWO

Thursday, 8:45 a.m.

WE RUN through Panera and end up sitting in the parking lot to eat breakfast and review Lisbeth's findings on Gilda Archer. It hit both of our inboxes late last night. Along with the DNA test that proves our homeless woman is indeed Natalie Catherine Scott, twin sister to Paige Bell.

Back to Gilda, there isn't much. Sixty years old. She once managed a strip club off I-40 passing through Knoxville. Before that, she worked the bar at the same strip club. And before that, she did odd jobs like fast food, a cashier at a convenience store, and waiting tables.

Vaughn's busy reviewing the same information. "Sixty? I would have placed her at seventy-plus."

In the world of strip clubs, there are the ones on the up and up, and the ones that deal under the table, offering other services. Her strip club was the latter, as evident by the number of times the place was busted for prostitution and drugs.

Somehow, though, she was never arrested. I also note she's owned the Iris Motel a little over a year.

Done reviewing the information, I put my phone away. "Cathy was a stripper. Maybe she worked for Gilda."

"I'd say that's a good guess."

"Cathy's life seems intertwined with Gilda and Twitch quite a bit. One of them has to know about Cathy's questionable influx of money that Rylan mentioned."

"It'll take some creative questioning to get Gilda to talk."

Rebecca appears in Vaughn's open window. It startles us both.

"You let him go." Her bruised bottom lip wobbles. "Why? He killed Cathy. You know he did."

Leaning down, Vaughn picks up a bag with a bagel sandwich that he bought for later. "Are you hungry?" he asks.

Despite the tears starting to appear, Rebecca nods. "I didn't go to Francis House for breakfast."

"Do you want to get in?"

"No. I can't be seen talking to you."

He looks around. "There's no one watching."

Rebecca hesitates, looking around as well.

Then she opens the back door, and with her oversized backpack, she slides in. Her body odor surrounds us. I lower all the windows. It helps a little.

Over the seat, Vaughn hands her the bag. We give her a few moments to eat.

I say, "Rebecca if you're willing to come forward about what Twitch did to you, we'll bring him back in."

She's already shaking her head before I finish the sentence. "Why did you let him go?"

"Because he had an airtight alibi. There's no way he

could have done it. But he's done so much more. If you and the other women that he's hurt are willing to ban together—"

Again, she's already shaking her head. "That's not happening."

"Then he'll continue to abuse you and the others."

"We know how to avoid him." She motions to her beat-up face. "This was my bad. I let my guard down. Plus, he has his favorites. I'm not one of them."

Vaughn shifts, looking more fully at her over the back seat. "Was Cathy?"

Rebecca nods. "I told her she didn't have to do anything, but she always said she didn't mind. 'We go way back,' she'd always say, like that even makes sense. He'd give her a five every blow. As long as she didn't fight him, he was gentle with her."

I feel sick.

"You've been in this area several months now. You came with Twitch and Cathy. Whose idea was it?"

"Twitch. His mother is Gilda over at the Iris Motel. He said she'd hook us up with money, food, and a place to stay." Rebecca snorts. "No thank you. I don't spread my legs for anybody. And I definitely don't give head. I'll stand on a street corner and beg before I do either of those."

"Did Cathy?" Vaughn asks.

"At the Iris Motel? All the time. But I don't judge. If that's how she wanted to make extra dough, more power to her."

"Can you think of anyone who was following you two? Or someone new that was suddenly friendly and talkative?"

Rebecca finishes eating. From her backpack, she finds a bottle of Coke and slurps several gulps. We wait patiently.

"Did you guys ever find Cathy's daughter?" she asks. "I'm thinking about moving on and really want to say hi, if I can."

It takes me a second to realize she's changed the subject. "We're still working on that."

Sadly, she smiles. "Maybe you could get me a copy of that picture of me and Cathy? All these years, and I don't have one. I'd love to give it to her daughter. I'd love to have one for myself as well."

"We can do that," Vaughn says. "If you decide to move on, make sure you find me and say bye."

With a nod, she opens the back door. She gets out and comes to stand at his window. "I said it was Twitch's idea to come here, but Preacher Mitch had a lot to do with it also. Me and Cathy knew him from another shelter back in Knoxville. He told us he was taking over Francis House and that if we were ever in the area, to look him up. It all kind of just came together when Twitch said his mom lived here."

She hoists the backpack up onto her shoulder. With a wave, she walks off.

Vaughn looks at me. "Preacher Mitch?"

"Let's do it."

TWENTY-THREE

Thursday, 9:45 a.m.

AT FRANCIS HOUSE, I walk past a few men and women sitting on the sidewalk. I make eye contact with each one, giving an acknowledging nod. One or two nods or smiles back.

Vaughn knocks on the locked red door. A moment later, Preacher Mitch answers, welcoming us in. "We're just cleaning up from breakfast," he says.

Unlike last time he doesn't lead us into his office. He stays standing in the entryway, silently letting us know he's busy and to make it quick.

Behind him down in the main room, several volunteers stuff paper bags with food.

"You didn't tell us you knew Cathy and Rebecca from before," Vaughn says.

"Yes. They frequented a shelter I worked at in Knoxville." He looks between us. "Since graduating seminary, I've worked at three different ones. I've seen a few of the same faces, Cathy and Rebecca being two of those."

"You arrived in this area not long before them. We understand you 'invited' them here. Is that usual?" I ask.

The preacher hesitates. "I work hard at bonding with all of my patrons. I care. If I see an opportunity, I make sure they know. Francis House is the best-equipped shelter I've worked at. I wanted them to know that. They're good women." Again, he looks between us. "What is going on?"

"How old are you?" Vaughn asks.

"Thirty-five."

"Have you always done this?"

Again, he hesitates. From down the hall where his office is located, a shadow shifts. "All done," comes a friendly female voice. Wearing her usual uniform of khakis and a blue polo, Destiny emerges, carrying a bucket of cleaning supplies. She comes up short when she sees us.

Preacher Mitch looks over his shoulder at her. "Awesome, thank you." He holds out a hand that she awkwardly takes. It's not a handshake; it's a sideways grasp like couples do. He squeezes her hand. "I'll see you later."

With a nod, she gives us a polite nod as she walks past us out the front door.

I give Vaughn a look and he nods, staying with the preacher so I can follow Destiny.

At a quick clip, she walks down the sidewalk and around Francis House where a parking lot sits with a couple of vehicles. She doesn't notice I'm behind her as she slides open the side of the van.

"Destiny," I say.

She looks up. "Um, I'm running late. I really can't talk."

"Are you doing okay?"

"Fine." She finishes loading the van, hurries around to

the driver's side, and nearly spits gravel as she quickly pulls away.

Interesting.

I backtrack, running into Vaughn. "She couldn't get away from me quick enough."

"She's been cleaning Francis House for years. Used to come with her grammy, always about this time."

"Between breakfast and lunch when the place is fairly empty. That explains why Cathy only saw her that one time. How long have Preacher Mitch and Destiny been an item?" I ask.

"He said they were just friends."

"Hm. Cathy asked everyone if they'd seen a young woman dressed in khaki pants and a blue top. How is it Preacher Mitch didn't know it was Destiny?"

"That I didn't ask. I didn't want to risk exposing Destiny's real identity and her link to Cathy. However, I got an answer about what he did before becoming a preacher."

"Please let it be good."

"He was in prison. I already texted Lisbeth for a thorough background on him." Sliding on his Ray-Bans, my partner walks toward the SUV.

Behind the wheel, I turn on the engine. I'm pulling away from the curb when my phone rings. It's Tyler. Over Bluetooth, I answer. "Hey, you're on speaker, what's up?"

He laughs at something someone just said. "Dad and Mom are here. We're making Mexican for lunch. Do you want to stop by?"

I both love and hate how happy he sounds. "You're supposed to be doing schoolwork."

"I will. Also, Mr. Bacote is here. He said he worked with Grandpa and that he's helping on a case you're working on. Anyway, should I tell him to meet you some-where or...?"

My brain scrambles to remember what I left out and put away. The file from Grandpa's shed is here in my SUV. "Are you on speaker?"

"No."

"Close the door to my room."

"I already did."

"Do not tell anyone that I store Grandpa's old files in our shed."

My brother's voice lowers. "I already did."

"Is the lock on the shed?"

"Yes."

"Don't give anyone the key. I'm on the way." I hang up.

"Do you not trust Captain Bacote?" Vaughn asks.

"I don't know. The only thing I do know is that my grandfather kept those files secret for a reason."

TWENTY-FOUR

Thursday, noon

AFTER DROPPING Vaughn at the station, I drive home. A tiny red Smart car is parked in our driveway. It's not the type of vehicle I expect a former detective to drive.

Inside the house, my mom and Tyler are in the kitchen laying out a Mexican-themed buffet complete with tortillas, a giant skillet of fajitas, refried beans, and all the sides. It smells heavenly.

In the living room, my father sits in the recliner that Grandpa always sat in and Captain Bacote sits on the old plaid couch. After I store my gun, I go to join them.

"I was in the area," Bacote says, answering my unspoken curiosity. "Our RV is parked over at Lazy Q's campground. Don't judge our tow-behind car." He laughs raucously. It reminds me of Sergeant Rogers' laugh.

Dad laughs right along with him.

I remain quiet.

"It's been forever since I was here." He looks around the

living room and kitchen separated only by a half wall. "Looks the same."

Mom says lunch is ready. We help ourselves to the Mexican buffet, resuming our seats in the living room to eat.

It takes exactly six minutes into our meal for Captain Bacote to say, "Nell, I was hoping to talk privately."

"Sure."

I remain quiet after that, idly listening to my family and Bacote chat, my brain spinning.

Sometime later lunch is done. Bacote and I step out into the sunshine. For the most part, I am an impatient person. I have questions and I need them answered. I am proactive. If there is a list to be done, I get it done. But with these types of things, I have infinite patience. I will stand for hours, silent, waiting for him to speak.

It only takes seconds.

"Any luck with identification on your homeless woman?"

This is going to be one of those conversations where he asks questions that he already knows the answers to. I'll play along. "Natalie Catherine Scott."

"All these years later. Interesting..." He glances away, squinting into the sun. "I hear you made an arrest, then let him go—David 'Twitch' Archer."

"Yes."

He looks away from the sun and back at me. "I hear you found the murder weapon."

"Yes."

"And that Gilda stepped forward with an alibi."

"Yes."

"I know Gilda from years gone by. She's a slick one. Don't underestimate her."

I nod.

"I hear you went to see Rylan Scott."

"Yes."

"What did he want?"

For me to give his daughter a letter. "More yard time before his execution."

Captain Bacote makes no expression. He knows I'm lying.

"Your brother mentioned that shed in the backyard has some of your Grandpa's old things. Tools, files, and whatnot."

"Yes."

"What kind of files?"

"Just personal stuff. Pictures. Notes on family trees. Old electric bills."

"Nothing about his old cases?"

"Not that I've seen."

"You'll let me know if you do see anything? We worked on a few things together over the years. I wouldn't mind adding his notes to mine."

"Of course."

"Okay. Well, the wife wants to shop Gatlinburg this afternoon. I better go. You've got my number."

I nod.

"Tell your parents I said thanks for lunch. I'm happy to see them together. That's something that concerned your grandfather."

Bullshit. Grandpa hated my dad. He would've never welcomed him back in.

Captain Bacote climbs into his toy car, starts the tiny engine, and drives off.

I text Vaughn.

Me: I need to move the files. Can I store them at your place until I figure something else out?

Vaughn: Of course. What did Bacote want?

Me: Cover his ass maybe? Rylan Scott was his last case.

Vaughn: And Bacote wants to make sure you don't put a kink in it.

Me: Anything back on Preacher Mitch yet?

Vaughn: Not yet. I was going to question Gilda without you but I figured you'd want in on the action.

Me: Correct. Be right there.

TWENTY-FIVE

Thursday, 1:45 p.m.

THE IRIS MOTEL is back in action with a few semitrucks parked in the lot, thick curtains closed on the windows, and Gilda sitting behind the still-clean counter smoking a cigarette.

I swing into the lobby with Vaughn right behind me.

Gilda's penciled eyebrows arch up. "Yes?"

"We hear you used to manage—" I look over at Vaughn — "What was the name of that again?"

"Bushes-R-Us."

"Ah, yes. Clever."

Vaughn trails his fingers down the brown footlong hot dog tie around his neck. "I was going to go with stupid."

"No, that tie is stupid," I say.

He looks at it like he's just seeing it for the first time. "You think so? I kind of like it."

Gilda glances at the fancy thin gold watch on her left

wrist. "If you're done with your little comedic routine, I'm busy."

On my phone, I pull up a ten-year-old photo of Cathy. "Did this woman used to work for you at Bushes-R-Us?"

Gilda barely looks at it. "Not that I remember."

I slap the counter. She jumps. I shove the phone under her nose. "Take. A. Better. Look."

She does, and while she's looking at the screen, I flip to the next picture—the one of Paige stabbed to death. Then the next—the one of Cathy stabbed to death.

Gilda flinches.

I say, "It's been ten years, but you don't strike me as the type to forget things. Like someone who worked for you. Like that same someone who was married to your son."

"Yeah, alright, I knew Natalie." Gilda shoves the phone away. "I told her she'd better behave. All that blackmailing she was doing would come back to bite her in the ass. It sure did."

My brows go up. "Bushes-R-Us had clients fancy enough to blackmail? The place doesn't exactly ring 'gentlemen's club'. I'd place it more as having a 'red light district' vibe."

"You'd be surprised at the fancy men *and* women who walked through those doors." Gilda straightens up like she's proud. "We were the only full nude show in town."

Vaughn leans an elbow on the counter. "Let me guess how this went down. You had Bushes-R-Us up and running. Out in the main area was the up-and-up stuff, if that's what you want to call it. In the back, you had rooms for other things. A little blow job here, a hand job there, penetration for extra, etcetera. What those back-room customers didn't know is that Natalie-slash-Cathy filmed the activity, especially if there was someone she knew she could circle back to and make a little blackmail cha-ching. Suddenly she had more money than she knew what to do with. You got pissed you didn't think of it. Then you decided—"

During Vaughn's speech, Gilda started filing her nails. She stops now. "Then I decided what? To kill her? To have her killed?" She laughs. "You were right on the blackmail, except she also sold the videos to a porn site. When I found out, I kicked her to the curb. I didn't care what happened to her. Still don't. But that doesn't mean I killed the wrong twin and then the right one.

"Her and Twitch kept in touch over the years. When he showed up here with her, I hadn't seen her since the day I threw her out on her ass. No love loss with that one. She looked like shit and I was happy to see it."

Gilda places her file down. Still seated, she looks up at us on the other side of the counter. "Listen, how about I give you that porn site in exchange for you leaving me alone."

"How about you give us that porn site, period," I say.

"Fine."

Back in the SUV, I say, "How did you know the black-mail route?"

"Back in Nashville, I was friends with a private investi-gator. Some fancy politician had this exact thing happen. He went into a back room at a strip club, got filmed, and later blackmailed. Talking to Gilda made me remember it all."

"We're keeping Lisbeth busy. Let's get that porn site to her." I turn on my engine.

Vaughn checks his phone. "A text came in from Destiny while we were in there with Gilda."

Destiny: Can you two meet me at the rest stop off exit 21?

TWENTY-SIX

Thursday, 3 p.m.

FROM THE IRIS MOTEL, we get on the interstate and drive ten miles to a rest stop with only one other vehicle parked near the restrooms—Destiny's van.

She sits at a concrete picnic table, waiting.

My partner and I sit down across from her.

"Interesting place to meet," I say, placing my grandfather's file on the table.

"I had a job nearby." She takes her white ball cap off and puts it to the side. "Sorry I was so weird earlier at Francis House."

"That's okay. What can we do for you?"

"I, um, googled Rylan, Natalie, and Mackenzie Scott." Nervously, she swallows. "I'm Mackenzie, aren't I?"

"Yes, we believe so. We would need a DNA sample before we say for sure."

This doesn't shock her as much as I thought it might.

She fiddles with her thumbnail. "I always thought something was weird. I have these odd memories of another life. Of a man pushing me on a swing. Of a woman sleeping on a couch. Of a couple fighting. Of someone sweet making cookies with me. Every time I brought it up, Grammy would change the subject. I guess I thought one day she'd tell me. Kind of like adoptive parents waiting for the right time to tell their kid she's not biologically theirs. Except Grammy died and here I am."

Destiny looks between us. "How did I come to live with Grammy?"

"Ten years ago you witnessed your aunt's murder. My grandfather believed your life was at risk. He facilitated your safety by placing you with your grammy. Your father pled guilty to protect you. Your mother took off. She is the woman who was found murdered in Memorial Gardens." I pause, giving her time to digest all of that. Then I say, "Destiny, we are concerned for your safety."

"Wow." She looks away, down to the grass beside the picnic table. "I witnessed it, but I wasn't able to remember who?"

"Yes. You were nine at the time and traumatized. You were mute. It took months for you to talk again."

She looks back up at me, and I'm hit again with how much her eyes look like her father's. "Should I do hypnosis or something?"

"Maybe," Vaughn says. "But we're on a tight timeline."

"You mean because my father is going to be executed?"

"Yes." I open the folder, taking out the drawing with the bold X's. "You drew this over and over again after seeing the murder. Do you—"

She gasps. She takes it from me. "I remember this. Oh my God. I remember this." Her hands tremble.

Gently, Vaughn says, "It's okay. Take your time."

"It's a tattoo." She grabs her upper right arm. "Right here. A row of X's circling the upper arm. The killer had that. I remember."

My heart surges. My grandfather's notes mentioned a tattoo. He suspected this. "Did you see a face?"

"Aunt Paige was in the kitchen. I was in the bath. Someone knocked. Then... screaming, so much screaming." She winces. "I got out of the tub. The door was cracked. I peeked through. My aunt was crawling away. The person followed her, stabbing and stabbing." She squeezes her eyes shut. "Dark jeans and white tennis shoes. A flannel shirt cut off at the shoulders. The X's. And a trucker's hat —like really big brimmed and roomy, pulled low. I was scared. I cowered behind the door. Then... silence. It was over. I don't remember hearing the person leave. I didn't move. I stayed cowered behind that door. For hours, I think. I remember Dad coming home. I remember cops arriving."

"The trucker's hat was pulled low. Do you remember a profile?" I ask. "A body build? Hair? Skin tone?"

Frowning, she looks away, thinking. "It was a white person, not black. Brown hair. It stuck out the bottom. The clothes were baggy, so I'd say the build was average. The person wasn't tall or short, again average, I guess. The face was clean-shaven." She nibbles her lip before looking back at us. "I think that's it."

"This is perfect, Destiny. Perfect." I stand up. "We're going to need you to come with us."

This alarms her. "*What*? Why?"

Vaughn holds a hand up. "It's okay. You're safe. We need a statement and a DNA test to prove you are Mackenzie Scott. That's all. It will allow us to file for a stay

of execution for your father, which is our number one prior-
ity. Then we'll be able to figure out who you saw."

"You're safe," I add.

TWENTY-SEVEN

Thursday, 5:30 p.m.

DESTINY NOW SITS in a private room while Vaughn and I meet with Sheriff Owens. I just told him everything, including showing him the file from my grandfather's shed.

It's been silent for the past several minutes as he thumbs through everything, digesting the details. Finally, he says, "We need to bring Captain Bacote in. He's the original lead on this."

I knew Owens was going to suggest that. "Sir, there is a reason why my grandfather kept much of this private, even from Captain Bacote, a longtime friend of his I might add."

Owens leans forward in his chair. Picking up a pen from his desk, he rolls it through his fingers, studying it for a few seconds. Then he looks across the desk at Vaughn. "Will you excuse us?"

With a nod, Vaughn does.

When the door is closed again, Owens says, "I'm always hesitant to speak about Sheriff Brach with you because of the fierce love you two shared. But Nell, I need you to hear me when I say, your grandfather was a hard man. Everyone knew not to cross him. He got results but didn't always make the best decisions. This made him human, sure, but what would have made him more human was that he could've owned up to things. He never did. Never once did he admit he was wrong. About anything. He would get things in his head and there was no reasoning with him. I could sit here and give you a long list to prove it, but I'm not going to do that. Instead, I am going to highly recommend you let me bring in Captain Bacote as a consultant and as a courtesy. This was his *solved* case. Ultimately, it's your decision. But if there is going to be a last-minute stay of execution, Bacote needs to be involved."

With a sigh, I glance over to the window that looks out over the workroom. Through the blinds, I see Vaughn busy at his desk. I also see Sergeant Rogers standing against the wall, drinking a bottle of water and staring right at me.

I turn back to Sheriff Owens. "We've got an audience."

As I had hoped Owens looks away from me and through the blinds straight at Rogers. Quickly, the sergeant makes himself busy.

Inwardly, I smirk.

"Okay." I push to my feet. "Let's bring in Captain Bacote. But I do not want Rogers involved. I know he used to work for Bacote and everything, but this isn't his case. He's in charge of domestic violence, yet he seems to pop up everywhere else."

"I'll make sure Bacote knows." The sheriff picks up his desk phone. "See to Destiny."

But when I walk the hall down to the room where we left her, she is gone.

TWENTY-EIGHT

Thursday, 6:30 p.m.

WE ISSUE A BOLO.

Vaughn and I split up. He checks her home. I go to Francis House, finding Preacher Mitch gone. I send Lisbeth a text:

Me: Do you have the background on Preacher Mitch yet?
Lisbeth: No, sorry. It's next on my list.
Me: Send it to me ASAP.

I spend time crisscrossing town, looking for her van. Night settles in, and with it, a text from Tyler:

Tyler: Dad wanted in the shed. Mom gave him the key. I didn't think you'd like that.

Given I haven't had the chance to move the files yet, I text back.

Me: On the way.

I make it home in record time.

Dad's car is still parked in the same spot as it was when I was home for lunch.

Through the living room window, I see Mom getting up from the couch and walking into the kitchen with a bowl. Tyler's probably in his bedroom. I walk right down the side yard to the back.

I find my father sitting at the table in the shed with my grandfather's files spread out. "What the hell are you doing?"

He jumps. "Your mom gave me the key."

I step forward and gather the files. "None of this is your business."

"I thought maybe some of it might belong to me."

I shove the files back into the box he opened. "Why would my grandfather have anything that belongs to you?"

"He wouldn't, I guess. I was just curious."

"No, you were being nosy. You want to know if Grandpa kept a file on you, don't you? Tell you what, if I find something with your name on it, I'll give it to you. Now get out of the shed. There is nothing in here that is any of your business."

With a heavy sigh, Dad steps out. I turn off the light, then shut and lock the door. I put the key in my pocket. I am moving these files tonight.

In the dark yard, I look at him. "How is it you are still here? Don't you have a job in Georgia to get back to?"

"I took the week off to be with my family."

I scoff.

"When are you going to cut me some slack, huh? I'm sorry I was a shitty father to you. But I'm here now and I want to make up for the lost time." He takes a step toward me.

"What are your plans, Dad? To marry Mom and take Tyler back to Georgia?"

He pauses.

My heart picks up pace.

"Well, your mom and I want to talk about all of that with you."

"Then talk. I'm listening."

"No, you're not. You're judging."

He's right I am. But when it comes to him, that's the only mode I know.

"We talked to an attorney," he quietly says. "With some paperwork and transfer of things, your mom will probably be allowed to leave the state."

"And Tyler?"

"Our lawyer feels we have a right to file for custody."

My muscles clench.

"But, Nell, we don't want that. We want to work things out peacefully with you. You know it's for the best. I mean, just look at the two of you. You're gone all day working. He's left at home to fend for himself. He needs more structure. He needs his father. He's thirteen. He'll be a man soon."

Dad has the whole lawyer-script down. "I know how old my brother is. I'm the one who has celebrated every birthday with him. Not you. Me."

"We talked to Tyler—"

My clenched muscles tighten even more.

"Everything okay?" Mom hesitantly asks.

I glance over to see her standing at the corner of the house. I hate that she looks so timid. She was doing so well until Dad stepped back onto the scene. Now she's back to being a little mouse. I want her to grow some balls.

But is she timid because of the way I'm acting or Dad?

I don't look at my father, I keep my focus on her. "If you wanted to work things out 'peacefully,' you wouldn't have gone to a lawyer." I'm going to regret the next words, but still, I say, "You are not taking Tyler. I will fight you. With everything I have, I will fight you. Now leave. Both of you."

AS SOON AS their taillights trail from the neighborhood, I dial my ex-lover and still friend, Judge Ronan Aaron.

He picks up on the second ring. "Nell."

I hear the smile in his voice. Despite everything going on with my parents, I smile back. "Ronan, thanks for picking up."

"Of course."

After we exchange a few catching-up pleasantries, I tell him what's going on with my parents and Tyler, finishing with, "Do they have a case?"

"You both do. From my standpoint, if I were the judge on this case, I would speak one-on-one with Tyler. He's old enough to weigh in. My ruling would be based on his input."

"I don't want to put him in a position to pick between me and our parents. He's doing so well. That would place unbelievable stress on him."

"If you go to court, it will be expensive and mean. Lawyers on both sides will drag everyone's names through the mud. Do you want that?"

"Of course not."

"Then you need to work this out with your parents."

We talk for a few more minutes, then I hang up. I get up from the kitchen table and as I do, I see Tyler standing in the archway that leads into the hall.

"You're fighting with Mom and Dad about me," he quietly says.

"And I thought you were nose-deep in a book or, better yet, homework."

"I was watching BBC on my iPad."

My brother loves British comedies. I wonder if my dad knows that.

Tyler moves around me, getting ice cream and a bowl. "Want some?"

"No, I'm good." Idly, I watch him scoop out vanilla—his favorite. Again, I wonder if Dad knows that. "Be honest with me; don't worry about hurting my feelings. I am a big girl. I promise. Tell me what you want. Where do you want to live?"

He stops scooping ice cream and looks at me. "I want Dad and Mom to get married. And I want all of us to move back to Georgia and be a family again. Can we do that, Nell?"

I stare into my brother's earnest gaze. His words are not what I wanted to hear, but for Tyler, I'll do anything. "Okay, let me talk to Mom and Dad. We'll see what we can work out."

TWENTY-NINE

Thursday, 9 p.m.

WITH FILE BOXES IN TOW, I knock on Vaughn's door.

He answers, still wearing his dark wash jeans from earlier, but down to just a white undershirt. He takes the box I'm holding and walks it into his apartment. "Nothing yet on the BOLO. But did you see the email from Lisbeth?"

"Not yet." The rest of the boxes I put on a small hand truck. I roll it in.

Vaughn continues, "Preacher Mitch was quite the thug. Did two of those scared-straight programs before he turned eighteen. No employment record until recently, which means everything he did was off the books. Did a stint in prison for assault with a deadly weapon, specifically a tactical knife. While he was inside, he saw the light. He's only been out for two years. He interned at two shelters, making Francis House his first actual posting. Used to go by Mitch Cowell, but changed it to Mitch Preacher when he got out. Wanted a fresh start, I guess."

"Preacher. How original." I unhook the bungee cord secured to the boxes and begin unloading.

Vaughn helps. "Ten years ago he was not in prison. He was still living the thug life in the Knoxville area."

"Motive?"

My partner grins. "Guess who his older brother is?"

"The president of the United States."

"Close. Knoxville's current chief of police."

"Now I'm excited."

Vaughn laughs.

I roll the hand truck back over to the door. "Okay, hypothetical time. Ten years ago, Preacher Mitch wouldn't have been someone to blackmail. But his presumably married cop-brother, soon-to-be-chief-of-police, yes. Big brother pays a visit to Bushes-R-Us. Gets filmed in the back room. Cathy then proceeds to blackmail him. Big Brother asks Little Brother to intercede. Little Brother's a thug. Sure, I'll do it. Why not? He shows up and kills the wrong twin. Fast-forward ten years and Little Brother becomes friends with the homeless woman, Cathy. He realizes who she is, as well as Destiny, and mentions it to Big Brother, who either sends someone to take care of her or gets Little Brother to do it. Though with Little Brother having turned over a new leaf, I vote for the former. You?"

"Hm. Or Big Brother threatened Little Brother. 'You make sure and tie up your loose ends or I'll make sure your life is shit.'"

"Please tell me Preacher Mitch has X's tattooed across his arm."

"Not really, but he does have one." Vaughn pulls a photo up on his phone. "This was taken years ago during his intake."

I zoom in. It's a simple black band circling his upper

right arm. "It might have been X's connected and colored in." I fish my keys from my pocket. "Put a real shirt on. Let's track down Preacher Mitch. And let's hope the BOLO produces Destiny."

THIRTY

AS WE CLIMB into my vehicle, I dial Mom. She picks up on the first ring. "Nell, please don't be mad."

"I don't have time to talk. Are you at Olivia's?"

"Yes, we both are."

Both, as in her and Dad.

"Can you stay the night with Tyler? We're down to the wire with this case."

"Of course. Be safe."

We hang up right as a text comes in from Captain Bacote.

Bacote: You did the right thing, bringing me in.

God, I hope so.

I KNOW AS SOON as we pull up to Francis House, that something's wrong. No lights are on and a line outside stretches around the block.

Still, I knock on the big red door.

"No one will answer," a homeless man says. "We're stuck out here for the night. Preacher Mitch didn't even open for dinner."

I knock again. Vaughn jiggles the door. In my peripheral I see Rebecca standing at the corner of the building. I turn fully to face her. She waves us over, and as we draw near, she steps around the building into the side parking lot.

Nervously, she looks past our shoulders making sure no one is listening. "I saw Preacher Mitch leave with a young woman. They got into a van. She was wearing khaki pants and a blue top. That's Cathy's daughter, isn't it?"

"When was this?"

"About six-thirty."

The last time I saw her was at the station before six. The timeline adds up.

"Did it look like there was a struggle?" Vaughn asks.

"No, but she seemed upset."

"Did you overhear anything?"

"Not really. Preacher Mitch got behind the wheel and she slid over to the passenger side. Then they drove away."

Just then both of our phones go off. Simultaneously we check the message. It's the BOLO.

The van's been found.

"Bring her home safe," Rebecca says. "Please."

THIRTY-ONE

Thursday, 11 p.m.

LOCATED next to a deserted convenient store, Destiny's van sits unlocked and open, still running, and with a large pool of coagulated blood gathering in the floorboards and smeared across the seats. The front bumper has a large indentation where it ran into something.

The sight of it punches into me. I pray Destiny is still alive.

Intermittent late evening traffic zips by on the nearby interstate. Other than a billboard advertising a new development going in miles down the road, there is nothing at this exit.

Forensics is already here working the scene. Vaughn stays with the van while I drive to the new development. A few spotlights illuminate the neighborhood with under-construction homes—only ten in all, none far enough along to have occupants.

With piles of building materials and a few trucks

parked for the night, the workers have all gone home. My headlights flash over mounds of dirt, stacks of bricks, large spools of wire, and piles of organized roofing material.

There is no one here.

Still, I grab my flashlight. Leaving my vehicle with the high beams directed at the construction zone, I walk through the stick-framed houses. With the construction not far along, it's easy to sweep my light across the rooms and floors.

It only takes me ten minutes to search the entire area.

As I'm climbing back in my vehicle, my phone rings. It's Vaughn.

"Anything?" he asks.

"No. The place is empty. I'll be back your way in a few minutes."

"Sounds good."

"Vaughn?"

"Yeah?"

"We've got to find her."

"We will."

I hang up and start the engine. From behind, a shadow shifts. I glance into the rearview right as someone presses a knife to my neck.

In the mirror, my eyes meet hers. Destiny. She looks terrified.

Her hand trembles. "Wh-where is your gun?"

"Right hip."

"H-hand it back." Her breath quivers. "Slowly."

I do.

She hesitates, unsure. "Your phone, throw it out the window."

I do that as well.

"D-do you have a radio?"

"Yes."

"Throw it out."

I comply.

She pants for breath. "Drive. Leave the neighborhood and go right, away from where I left the van."

I swallow, feeling my throat scrape the blade. "Destiny, I can't drive with that on my neck."

Nodding, she puts the knife aside and picks up the gun. She takes the safety off and points it at me. Again, her hand trembles. "I know how to use this. Grammy taught me."

"I believe you."

She slides back, sitting in the center, and points the gun at the back of my seat. "Drive."

I hate that my hands shake as I put the vehicle in drive and pull from the neighborhood, going right as she said. "My partner will know something is wrong if I don't return."

She makes no response.

Over the years I've been a cop, I've learned that fine line that delineates when a person has stopped caring. When they feel they have no hope. Destiny has not crossed that line. But she's close. She's petrified. I have to proceed carefully.

I look at her in the rearview, seeing for the first time blood on the front of her shirt and smeared on her arms and neck. "Are you hurt?"

"It's not my blood."

"Whose is it?"

"Mitch's." Her voice cracks. "I-I killed him. Or at least I think I did."

"In self-defense?"

"I don't know. Maybe?" She holds up a large tactical knife, but it's not a folding one. "With this. He had it in his things. I found it. I asked him about it. But he didn't answer me. He just told me to calm down. It's just like the ones used to kill my aunt and mother, right?"

"Not quite, but close."

"No," she groans.

I focus on maintaining a calm voice. "Destiny, start from the beginning. The last time I saw you, you were at the station. What happened?"

"Mitch and I, we've become friends over the past months. Good friends. We've talked a lot, ya know? All I wanted to hear was his voice. So, I called him. And then I was telling him about how I witnessed a murder a long time ago and how I've been living under a different name and that you all wanted a statement. But I didn't use names. I never once told him who my father and mother are. Or who I am. H-he told me to leave. He said that he would protect me. That I needed a lawyer if you were going to question me. He said I was in danger.

"At first, I didn't move from that room you put me in. Then I opened the door, looking for you. Instead, I saw this old man and I remembered him. He questioned me a long time ago. Suddenly, I was nine again and scared. I panicked. I ran from the police station. I met Mitch at Francis House. I was so shaken up, I couldn't even drive. We went to my place and packed a bag. He was going to take me to his brother. He's the chief of police in Knoxville. Mitch said if anyone had the resources to protect me, it was his brother.

"We got about thirty minutes down the road and he started talking about how he used to be in prison. He said he'd done bad things. Then something about him changed. He became even calmer. He asked me if I remembered the killer's face. He told me he knew Cathy was my mother and

Rylan my father. He knew who *I* was. I freaked. *How do you know that?* I shrieked. *I didn't tell you that!*

"He just kept telling me to calm down. But every time he said that I got more and more panicked. *You're misunderstanding me,* he said. *I knew who your mother was all along. She told me about her past. I kept it private. When she told me she saw her daughter, I knew immediately it was you. But I also knew to keep that a secret as well.* Then I found the knife in his things and I full-on freaked. I started yelling. *Let me out! Let me out!*

"But he wouldn't. He just kept telling me to CALM DOWN. He tried to take the knife from me and I stabbed him. Twice, I stabbed him. Both times in the neck. The van veered off the road and ran into a tree. I opened the door and pushed him out. I drove off. And I kept driving and driving, and somehow I was back in White Quail. I don't even remember turning around. I stopped the van, and I ran."

Her scared eyes meet mine. I'm glad to still see the fear. I can work with fear. It's when that leaves and vacancy enters that the situation becomes no return.

The road darkens the further we get from civilization. I don't know where this road goes. But my headlights slice through the night picking up endless trees on both sides with an occasional house tucked in.

"I-I killed him."

"You don't know that."

"I do. There was so much blood." Her breath quickens. "So much. The worst part is, the more I think about it, the more I don't think Mitch was a bad guy."

"You don't know that either."

"I do. He was just trying to help. And now he's dead.

DEAD. I killed him! Which means the real bad guy is still out there."

"Destin—"

The gun comes up. She points it at my head. "Shut up! Drive."

My heart picks up speed, thumping hard in my chest. I concentrate on the road, trying desperately to ignore the gun at my head. She told me to be quiet, but my gut says to keep going. My words come quiet, "I promised your father that I'd keep you unseen and safe. Let me live up to that promise."

"Unseen?" She scoffs. "Little late for that, don't you think?"

Shit, I picked the wrong word.

Her lips press together, the bottom one unsteady. For several seconds she keeps the gun pointed at my head. Then she slides back to her spot in the center and lowers the weapon.

I keep driving. "Where are we going?"

"I don't know. As far as this road will take us, I guess. I'm sure eventually we'll see blue lights flashing behind us. Until then, just drive. I need to think."

"Destiny—"

"I *said*, drive. I need to think. Don't speak. Do you hear me? Don't."

I nod.

THIRTY-TWO

Thursday, 11:45 p.m.

I KEEP WINDING FURTHER and further down the dark country road. My lights catch on a few mailboxes. A couple of vehicles pass me going in the opposite direction. It's not often I wish we lived in a big city, but right now I do. Rural Tennessee can be desolate.

Occasionally, I glance in the mirror. Destiny doesn't make eye contact. She simply stares out the front window, watching me drive. The gun remains pointed at my back.

Up ahead some lights come into view. We're entering a small town. I read the name on the sign, Richie Cove. We're still in our county.

In the distance, a train's horn sounds. Up ahead the crossing bar blinks and lowers. I half expect her to tell me to run it, but she doesn't. Other than the approaching train and a gas station closed for the night, there is nothing else on this side of the tracks. The rest of the small town is up ahead.

Behind us, faint blue lights illuminate the darkness. I stop the vehicle.

Destiny opens the back door and steps out. "Let's go. Keep your hands where I can see them."

"We're not even sure if Mitch is dead."

"I said let's go." She points the gun at me.

With my hands in the air, I do what she says. We walk away from the car, across the two-lane road, and past the gas station. Darkness engulfs us. I lead. She follows. The nearly full moon gives us the only light. The train gets closer. Sirens pulse through the night. It won't be long until Vaughn finds us.

"It doesn't matter," she says. "If Mitch is dead I'll go to prison. If he's alive, I still go to prison for stabbing him. Everyone will officially know who I am. Whoever's wanted me dead all these years will finally do it. Hell, I'll probably be shanked in jail."

"I can protect you."

"Really?" She jabs the gun in my back. "Who's the hostage right now? And you want me to trust you to protect me? Oh, yeah, add this to my jail time. Kidnapping a cop. Great."

Gone is the fear in her voice to be replaced by cynicism. The switch is not good.

Another horn from the train. The ground vibrates beneath my feet.

Running footsteps come from behind us. "Drop the weapon!" Vaughn shouts.

"Just do what he says," I plead. "I'll help you through this. I promise. Trust me, Destiny."

The wind around me kicks up. The train barrels past, deafening the air. I look over my shoulder. My stomach pitches when I see the wildness in her gaze. She's a step away from losing control.

Jabbing the gun further into my back, her fingers dig into my shoulder and she turns me to face Vaughn. In the distance, more blue lights make an appearance.

"Let her go!" Vaughn barks.

The gun trembles.

I raise my hands in a calming gesture. "It's going to be okay, Destiny."

"Stop saying that!" she screams. "Did you find Mitch?" she shouts over the passing train. "Is he dead?"

Vaughn doesn't respond.

"TELL ME."

"Yes, we found him." He keeps his gun focused. "Yes, he's dead."

"No," she whimpers.

"Things aren't as bad as you think," I say. "We're good people. Let us help you."

The gun leaves my back. She points it straight up and fires. I duck and swerve, coming down hard on her right arm. She howls in pain. The gun lands at my feet.

Destiny runs.

"Stop!" Vaughn yells, about to fire his gun.

"Don't shoot her!" I shout.

I take off after her, running with the train. Vaughn goes left to cut her off in the bordering trees. She races into the dark. The ground slopes gently down. At the bottom, the tracks veer left. She'll be trapped.

We've got her.

The sound of my soles hitting the grass comes light, but my pace is anything but as my legs propel me forward.

The train keeps coming, it's a long one.

Destiny stumbles. She looks back.

"Destiny!" I yell, almost catching up. "Please."

She digs in, going even faster. I'm in good shape, but this girl can run.

My chest heaves. I gauge the distance between us and where the tracks veer. About fifty yards to go, and we'll have her. I look left. I don't see Vaughn. I hear her sob. The desperation in it tears through me.

The train's horn echoes one last time. It's almost passed us. The ground rumbles. I spy Vaughn up ahead, coming from the trees.

In my peripheral, the end of the train comes into view. Destiny's speed increases even more. Her hair flies.

She's going to try and run across the tracks after it passes.

I wave at Vaughn, letting him know I've got her. There are only ten yards between us. My gaze bounces from her to the end of the train and back to her. She's going to have to stop. She's running too fast.

But she doesn't stop.

She runs at full speed, straight into the train.

THIRTY-THREE

Friday, 3 a.m.

MY MOVEMENTS ARE robotic as I file paperwork, give a statement, and talk to Sheriff Owens.

In a daze, I walk from the station and over to my vehicle. After I get behind the wheel, I look in the rearview, imagining Destiny back there. I go through the entire night, forward and backward. There are so many things I could've done differently—words I should've said, actions if taken may have turned the events.

I wanted to help her. I believed I would be able to. I thought we would both walk away alive. But she's dead.

Because of me.

Preacher Mitch did not kill Paige Bell. Sure he was still a thug ten years ago, living in Knoxville. But the week Paige died, he was in the hospital having surgery on a broken leg.

If Lisbeth would've found that information sooner...

No, don't do that, Nell. This is on you. No one else.

Any chance of saving the one last life in this—Rylan

Scott—is gone. He's going to die later today because of my inability to solve the case and the mishandling of this investigation.

Now I'm faced with telling him his daughter is dead.

He had one dying request, and I can't make it happen.

I put my vehicle in gear and drive from the lot, but I don't go home, I go to Vaughn's apartment.

His light is on. I knock on the door. He opens it. I take one look at his tired and distraught face and I lose it. He opens his arms. I step into them.

And I cry.

THIRTY-FOUR

Friday, 7:15 a.m.

I SLEEP at Vaughn's on the couch. When I wake up, I check in with Mom.

"Sorry to be out all night," I say. "It was a... bad night."

Her voice is soft. "It's okay. We're doing fine here. I work the morning shift at Starbucks. Your father is going to stay with Tyler."

"Thanks."

As much as I hate to admit it, it's comforting they were able to help.

With one last thank-you, I hang up. Charlotte arrives. She doesn't bat an eye at my being here. She jumps right into the kitchen, making breakfast for the three of us.

He brings me black coffee. "No coconut milk here. Sorry."

"That's okay."

He sits beside me on the green fabric couch. Silently, I drink my coffee while he sips his usual tea.

"This is on both of us," he says. "Know that, okay?"

I don't respond.

"We still have that porno site that Lisbeth's working on. There might be a familiar face. We're not done."

"We both know Rylan is innocent. Even if by some miracle we get that stay of execution, the only thing he loved is now gone." *Because of me.* Proving his innocence is the only thing left to make all of this right. "I'm going into the city later. I need to face him when I deliver the news about his daughter."

"I'll go with you."

"No, I want to go alone."

"Okay."

Charlotte walks in from the kitchen carrying two plates with eggs and bacon. Despite my shitty mood, it smells heavenly and sparks my hunger.

She hands me a squeeze bottle of yellow mustard. "I heard you eat this on everything."

"Thanks." I sit my coffee down, cover the eggs with my favorite condiment, and eat.

Charlotte tries to make small talk, but I'm not in the mood. Vaughn gives his best effort to reciprocate her efforts, but even that comes across as stilted. Eventually, she gives him a kiss and leaves.

When the door closes behind her, I say, "I'm sorry. She's sweet. She always sees my bitchy side though."

"No, I told her we had a crappy night. She came here knowing it would probably be like this."

After eating the last bite of egg, I put my plate down. "I'm happy for you with her."

"Thanks." He picks up my plate and takes both into the kitchen.

"Why do you care so much about the homeless?" Seemingly, the question comes out of nowhere but I have been wondering.

"Because that was me and my mom." He comes back into the living room, sitting again on the couch. "We slept many a night in her old car. There's so much stigma around that population. They're lazy. Stop standing by the curb holding up a sign. Just go get a job. Etcetera. It's not like anyone chooses to be homeless. There are a lot of circumstances that lead to it. I'm one of the lucky ones. I kept going to school despite the fact I hadn't showered in days. I made good grades. I had teachers who cared. I held down a full-time job. I managed to get us into a tiny apartment. I snagged a scholarship to college. We turned our lives around. Fast forward and my mom is happy and healthy. She works at Sephora, which is perfect for her. She's quite the diva. Makeup is her jam." He grins.

I smile. It feels good to do so. Only minutes ago, I didn't have one in me. "You are amazing, Vaughn London."

He toasts his mug to mine. "Back at ya, Nell Brach."

THIRTY-FIVE

Friday, 9 a.m.

FROM VAUGHN'S PLACE, I run home for a shower and a change of clothes. I'm right on the dot when I pull into the station's lot. My partner stands beside his Mini Cooper speaking with Rebecca.

Today he wears a florescent blue tie with a funny chicken. Too bad we're not in a nightclub because he'd glow in the dark.

"I was just about to text you," he says, nodding to Rebecca.

"Is it true?" she mumbles. "Is Cathy's daughter dead?"

"Yes," I say.

"And Preacher Mitch?"

"Yes."

Rebecca's eyes tear up. "I liked Preacher Mitch."

"I'm sorry," I quietly say.

As quickly as her tears arrived, they disappear. She

becomes angry. "Twitch did Cathy. I'm sure of it. I haven't seen it, but I heard he's walking around with a Polaroid of her dead body. Not like from the morgue or something. She's right there in the woods. How did he get that?"

Vaughn and I exchange a glance.

My phone rings. It's the station's receptionist.

I step away to answer. "Detective Brach here."

"There's someone in the lobby asking for you. She works out at the truck stop. Says she has information regarding Gilda and this past Sunday."

"I'll be right in."

I leave Vaughn talking with Rebecca and step inside the lobby to find a young heavyset woman sitting on a bench. She stands when she sees me. "Detective Brach?"

"Yes." I shake her hand.

"I'm Betsy. I work the register out at the truck stop diner. I worked on Sunday. I heard some cops were asking around about Gilda and Twitch being there Sunday afternoon. They were, but Twitch left at five. Gilda stayed and had pie and coffee. She left an hour later. He bought cigarettes from me, walked right out, got in Gilda's car, and drove away. When Gilda left, she grabbed a ride from a trucker she knows. He took her back to the Iris Motel. Full disclosure, I cannot stand either one of them. I would love nothing more than to see them go down for something, *anything*. But I'm not making this up. I'm telling the truth. I know this is about that murdered woman at Memorial Gardens. Twitch had plenty of time to drive over there and do it."

"Betsy, this is a big help. I'm going to have someone take an official statement."

She nods.

I get her settled with a uniformed officer and I walk back outside to see Rebecca walking away.

Quickly, I tell my partner what Betsy just said. "Looks like we're circling back to Twitch."

THIRTY-SIX

WE PULL into the Iris Motel. Like the first time we were here, an old white four-door is parked at the end of the lot.

Vaughn walks toward the front office. I stay standing near my SUV. He opens the office door. I hear more than see Gilda sigh.

"What now?" she snaps.

"We're looking for your son," he says.

I'm surveying the exterior of the rooms—some with open curtains, others with closed—when the door at the very end flies open and a wiry man erupts.

"Stop!" I yell.

Twitch disappears around the corner of the motel.

I go into a full sprint, straight across the lot. I make it to the end of the motel, hang a right, and follow his path into the trees.

My feet hit an unexpected decline and I slide down a

hill. Branches whip at me. I hiss. Gravity pulls me and I get back on my feet, nearly running in the air. Something flicks to my right. I catch sight of Twitch scurrying through a lone beam of sunlight. Scrubs and branches block the route in front of him. He curses, getting tangled up. The trees open up to the gravel service road.

Cutting a diagonal path, I thunder through the last bit of pines, swing around a trunk, and plow feetfirst into him.

We go down hard where the trees meet the gravel road. I grab Twitch's arm and he swings out. His knuckly fist connects with the bone just beneath my eye. Pain explodes through my skull. *Son of a bitch!* I make another grab for him and he kicks me in the ribs—once, hard.

The trees spin. Nausea climbs my throat. My vision blurs.

I blink, just making out Twitch scrambling away. He stumbles around a bend in the service road. A shadow moves. But Twitch doesn't see it. He's too busy looking back at me. From the other direction, Vaughn collides with him. There's a shout, a thrown fist, a grunt. Twitch goes down.

"Get the fuck off of me!" he shouts.

Vaughn pushes him into the gravel and cuffs him.

With a groan, I look up at the sky, taking in some deep breaths.

By the time I stand and make it down the gravel road, my partner has Twitch on his feet. I come to a stop, getting right into his personal space. My face darkens.

He glares.

I tap my cheekbone where his fist connected. "Not a good idea." Then I throw a punch of my own. Right into the spot under his eye that will mirror mine.

He yelps. "You're not allowed to do that!"

"Do what?" I look at Vaughn. "What did I do?"

My partner smooths a hand over his uncharacteristically rumpled hair. "Nothing that I saw."

"David Archer, you are under arrest for the murder of Natalie Catherine Scott."

THIRTY-SEVEN

Friday, noon

WITH A BRUISE rapidly forming under my eye, I sit across from Twitch. Vaughn occupies the chair beside me. Directly behind us stands a video recorder. Beyond that is the two-way mirror where Sheriff Owens and Captain Bacote are watching.

Twitch said he didn't want a lawyer. Translation: he thinks that will make him look innocent. His gaze stays fixed on the table between us. Like me, a bruise is forming under his eye. It gives me a modicum of gratification.

I wait impatiently, arms folded, foot tapping against the tile floor.

I didn't say a word, I simply placed the evidence bag on the table with a Polaroid of Cathy's freshly stabbed body that we found in Twitch's things at the Iris Motel.

That was five minutes ago. He's been staring at it ever since.

Finally, he raises his gaze to meet mine. "I don't know how I have that."

"Then why run? Why resist arrest?" I show him my bruised cheek. "That's a lot of bad decisions for such an innocent man."

"Because you all have it out for me."

My tapping foot settles. Linking fingers on top of the table, I lean forward. My voice lowers. "Heard you been forcing some of the homeless women around here into 'servicing' you." I click my tongue. "Gosh, between that, the murder weapon we found on you, and this Polaroid, I don't even know where to start with all we plan on charging your sorry ass with."

Twitch shoots Vaughn a desperate look that he calmly ignores.

I push Cathy's photo forward. "Gilda's been your alibi quite a bit, hasn't she? See, the problem is we have an eyewitness that puts you leaving the truck stop and driving off in Mommy's car. Plenty of time for you to go to Memorial Gardens and take out Cathy. What, was she getting on your nerves? Were you finally sick of her? You really thought burning her fingers and pulling her teeth would put a hiccup in our investigation?"

Next, I place a photo of Twitch's tattoed upper body on the table. I point to his upper right arm, covered in so much old and new art, it's impossible to make any of it out. "You have a lot going on here, makes me wonder if you're covering old things."

Slowly, Twitch's agitation rises. Breathing heavily in and out of his nose, he scrubs ten dirty fingers through his bushy gray beard. I keep quiet. Now is the time to let the silence worm its way into his head.

I keep staring at him, waiting for the moment. That moment when the gravity of the situation hits full force.

It doesn't take long.

His breathing shallows out. Tears shimmer. His bottom lip wobbles.

Here we go.

Twitch sniffs. "I want to talk to my mom," he whispers.

I sit back. I was not expecting that.

"Please," he sobs.

My palm smacks the table. Twitch jumps. "Gilda?" I scoff. "You don't have the right to see your mother."

A knock comes on the door. Sheriff Owens opens it. He doesn't say a word, just nods us out.

I lean in. Twitch cowers away. It doesn't bring me nearly as much satisfaction as it should.

THIRTY-EIGHT

Friday, 1:30 p.m.

ON THIS SIDE of the two-way mirror, I stand in a row with Captain Bacote, Vaughn, and Sheriff Owens. Gilda was already at the station, arrested for obstruction of justice. If it were up to me, there is no way these two would be talking. But Owens and Bacote wanted to see how they interacted. So, here we are.

I left the photo on the table.

Both are handcuffed. Gilda is currently staring at the photo while Twitch cries. That's all he's been doing. At first, I thought he was faking it, but no one can fake that many tears and that much snot.

The door opens to our room. Sergeant Rogers steps in. He takes one look at my face. "Nice shiner," he says.

I wait for the sheriff to tell him to leave, but he doesn't. He remains focused on mother and son.

"I can't believe I'm handcuffed," she spits. "All these years and I've never been arrested. Now I am, and for what?

A lying sack of shit son? You told me you wanted to run errands. I believed you. I lied for you."

"I don't know how I have that picture, Mommy. I swear. Someone is setting me up. I did run errands. Remember I returned with bags of stuff? Even things you needed. Remember?"

"Yeah, after you butchered Cathy. I never did like her, but Jesus, no one deserves how she died." Gilda shifts forward. "They found the murder weapon on you." She looks over at the mirror. "Which I also lied about. You might as well know. I didn't find it in my dumpster."

"Someone's setting me up," he cries. "I'm being framed."

She scoffs. "Like I haven't heard that a million times over the years."

His crying increases.

Gilda sighs, heavy and deep. A few quiet seconds roll by. Shaking her head, she looks back down at the photo of Cathy's body. "I haven't been the best mother. I was so proud when you joined the military. I thought, hell, I must have done something right. I bragged on you. I told everyone my boy had joined up. 'Course you came back a lot sooner than I expected. But whatever. I was still proud."

Her voice breaks. "I would do—*have* done—anything for you. But this? I'm not the mother of a murderer. I won't be. I never thought I'd say this, but I regret us mending fences. We're done. I don't know what's going to happen to me, but don't ever contact me again."

"No," he sobs.

"You've been nothing but a pain in my ass." Gilda looks over at the mirror. "Let me out."

"We've got the murder weapon, the photo, and a recanted alibi." Sheriff Owens cups a hand on my shoulder.

"Good work." He looks between me and Vaughn. "Both of you. We've got the man who killed Natalie Catherine Scott."

As he leaves the room, Captain Bacote looks at me, his gaze touching my bruised eye.

"I want to file for a stay of execution," I say.

"It's too late. Rylan's being executed tonight."

"It's not too late. We have Destiny's testimony."

"No, you don't. She never made an official statement."

"We have Twitch."

"Who you've nailed for Cathy. He didn't do Paige."

"But—"

Captain Bacote takes a calm breath. "I understand the frustration. Yes, the murders are similar, but they are not exact. It would have been easy for Twitch to mimic what was done with Paige. The same type of knife, with the same stabbing pattern. Happens all the time. It's called copycatting."

"Sir—"

"Be content with catching this one. Rylan admitted to Paige."

My stomach cinches tight. I'm not ready to give up on linking the two kills.

"Will you at least consider filing for that stay? Vaughn and I both heard what Destiny said. We'll swear to it." I look at Vaughn.

"Yes," he says.

Captain Bacote takes a few seconds, looking back and forth between us. "Okay, but I'm not making any promises."

"Thank you, Sir. Thank you."

He leaves with Sergeant Rogers following closely behind.

After the door closes, I glance at Vaughn who is watching Twitch be escorted from the room.

He says, "I hate to say it, but I think I believe him. Someone's framing him."

"I agree."

THIRTY-NINE

Friday, 3 p.m.

IN OUR STATION'S small press room, Sheriff Owens is currently making a statement. "Thanks to the excellent police work of Detective Nell Brach and Detective Vaughn London, we have arrested the man who..."

Captain Bacote is in there listening along with several others.

I sit at my desk, idly staring at the crayon sketch Destiny did years ago. It's the one piece of evidence I thought would be my smoking gun. Instead, it's a talisman for my inability to save Rylan Scott's life.

Across from me, Vaughn sits at his desk, flipping through the porno site Gilda gave us. Lisbeth already combed through it but saw no one of interest. Her only comment was, *Ick.* Anybody who would be of interest likely paid the blackmail money so their amateur porn wasn't posted.

Vaughn doesn't glance up from the laptop. "Have you ever been to an execution before?"

"No."

"Me neither. Rylan's going to look out though and see a comforting face."

I frown. "I never said I was going to his execution."

"Oh, I just assumed."

"No, I am going to speak with him, though. I need to tell him about Cathy and Destiny."

"Are you sure?"

"What do you mean?"

"Do you want the last hours of his life to be about grieving his wife and daughter? *Especially* the daughter. He wanted to write a letter to Destiny. Let him do it. It'll be good for him."

Like earlier, my stomach pitches. I'm not sure about that. Feels wrong.

Still staring at the laptop, Vaughn straightens. He clicks the laptop, rewinds, and then plays the video in slow motion. "Holy shit. Shit. Shit. Shit. Get over here."

He zooms in on a girl. She might be topless and wearing a thong, but she does not look of age. With long auburn hair parted and styled into two pigtails, she's in the middle of giving a blow job.

Vaughn freezes the frame, zooming in more. A row of X's encircles her upper arm. He looks up at me. "We've been looking for a man this whole time. That's not a man."

"No, it is not." I click print. "Let's find out who that is."

FORTY

SITUATED BACK IN AN INTERROGATION ROOM, Gilda sits handcuffed across from me. I show her the photo of the girl in pigtails. "Who is this?"

She doesn't even look at it. "If I look at that and can help, what do I get in return?"

I don't hesitate. "For obstruction, you'll likely get one year. We'll knock it down to six months plus probation."

"I want it in writing."

"You'll have to trust me. We don't have time."

She nods to the picture. "Let me see."

I slide it over.

"That's Skye," Gilda says. "She lived with Cathy and Rylan for a while. Cathy brought her to me. I put her to work. She was popular in the back rooms."

"She doesn't look much past thirteen," Vaughn says.

"Exactly. She appealed to the pedophiles. Her ID said

eighteen, so don't go thinking you can slam me with that charge in addition to whatever else."

"Was Skye caught up in the blackmail mess?" I ask.

"Yes, but not like you think. It wasn't the men she serviced, it was her father. He was a big businessman in Knoxville. Had a lot of money. He paid time and again so Cathy wouldn't sell the porn. Looks like she did anyway."

"What was his name?" I ask.

"Don't know. That girl though overdosed. She's long been dead."

"What about that tattoo on her upper arm?"

Gilda shrugs. "No clue."

WE FIND Lisbeth and give her the photo of Skye. We tell Lisbeth everything that Gilda said. "Any chance you can fill in the gaps? We need to know who her father was."

"I'll give it my best shot."

The lobby receptionist passes us, having just arrived for her shift. Carrying a lunch box and purse, she's on her way to the break room. She pauses at Lisbeth's desk. "Detective Brach, did you get all those messages yesterday evening?"

"What messages?"

"From that young woman who jumped in front of the train. I was working the desk last night. She called here several times. I gave the notes to Rogers to give to you."

"Why did you give them to Rogers?"

"He was passing through the lobby on his way back here and said he'd give them to you." Hesitantly, she frowns. "Did you not get them?"

My fingers curl into two fists. I turn away.

"Nell." Vaughn grasps my arm. "What are you doing?"

I search the workroom busy with activity. My gaze lands on Rogers, standing on the other side of the room beside Captain Bacote. Rogers erupts with his annoyingly loud laugh. He slaps his thigh.

My feet move forward. I weave my way through the desks and people busy working. Behind me, I only slightly register Vaughn following, speaking my name.

A few uniformed officers glance at me as I pass. With his stupid-ass Cheshire grin, Rogers looks over right as my fist comes back and I punch him straight in the nose.

The room falls silent.

Captain Bacote steps between us. He pushes a hand against my shoulder. "Enough."

Behind him, Rogers sputters and cusses. Sheriff Owens erupts from his office.

I take a step back, pointing my finger at Rogers. "Don't you ever keep messages from me again. That girl is dead. *Me*, she was trying to reach me, not you. *Me*. I could have saved her life if I had gotten those messages."

"You don't even know what's on them," he snaps.

"It doesn't matter!" I shout.

"I was going to give them to you. It's not like I kept them on purpose." He presses the back of his hand to his nose. "Jesus, I'm bleeding."

"Where are they?" I demand.

"On my desk." He looks over at the sheriff. "You gonna let her get away with that?"

Sheriff Owens makes no reply.

Rogers pushes past Bacote and charges over to the bathroom.

I about-face and go to Sergeant Rogers' desk. Gradually, the room becomes active again. I don't look at the sheriff. I'm in trouble. I'm fully aware of this.

I find the yellow memo messages taken down by the receptionist. Four total.

Message #1 (Thursday 6:30)
I lost your card. Please call me.
Message #2 (Thursday 7:45)
I'm with Mitch. Please call me.
Message #3 (Thursday 9:05)
I'm scared. Please call me.
Message #4 (Thursday 10:25)
Oh, God. I did something bad. Please help.

I am so mad I can't think.

I find the receptionist in the break room putting away her things. "Hey!"

She jerks.

"Nell," Vaughn quietly says. "Not here."

"The next time anyone, and I mean *anyone* calls here and asks for me, you find me." I pin her with my angry gaze. "Never give the message to someone else. Do you understand?"

She gives an erratic nod. "Yes. I'm sorry."

I'm taking this out on her, but I seriously am about to lose it.

Behind me, Vaughn says, "If you're going to see Rylan, you have to leave now. I'll manage things on this end. We still have time."

FORTY-ONE

Friday, 5 p.m.

UNLIKE THE LAST time I came here, this time a Plexiglas wall separates me from Rylan Scott in a small room. When the guard put me in here, he told me it was because we were in the last hours of Rylan's life.

There's a nervous energy about him that wasn't present before. It vibrates off of him. I'm sure if there wasn't a wall between us, I would feel it pulsing the air around me.

They took the cuffs off of him when they put him in the room. His hands shake as he balls them into fists and presses them into his thighs.

Several holes perforate the barrier. He leans toward them. "Thank you for coming."

On the way here, I made myself calm down. And I decided that Vaughn is right. Rylan's last hours shouldn't be spent grieving the loss of a daughter. It doesn't matter that I'm the reason why. I won't relieve my guilt and unburden my soul if it means this man will suffer any more than he already is.

Rylan deserves me strong and in control. "Did you write the letter for your daughter?"

"Not yet. I was waiting to hear if you'll be able to give it to her."

"Write it," I say.

His smile is wobbly. "Okay."

"I wonder if you can tell me about a girl named Skye. She used to live with you and Cathy."

"Oh, wow. That's a name I haven't thought of in years. Yeah, we let her crash on our couch for a while. She was just a kid, probably like fifteen, if that. Ran away from home. She was sweet. Used to sing Mackenzie to sleep at night."

Something tells me he doesn't know Skye got caught up in Cathy's schemes. "Do you know her last name?"

"No."

"She had a tattoo on her upper arm." I grasp my right one. "Here. It was a row of X's. Any idea what that meant?"

"Yeah, I asked her that. She said it was a warning not to mess with her. Wait a minute... is that what Mackenzie drew with the X's?"

"Yes. I find it curious though that a teen girl would have that kind of tattoo."

"She said she stole the idea off of someone but didn't tell me who. I wonder what happened to Skye. She'd be around twenty-five now."

She overdosed, but like so many other things, I keep that to myself.

He draws in a breath and it visibly soothes him. "I'm going to go write that letter."

FORTY-TWO

Friday, 6:05 p.m.

IN THE PRISON WAITING ROOM, I dial Vaughn. I recap the conversation I had with Rylan, ending with, "Skye stole the tattoo idea from someone else. That person—whoever it is—is the one Destiny saw. That person did both Paige *and* Cathy. I know it."

"Does Rylan know you're trying for a stay?"

"No, he specifically asked me not to. I'm lying to him about so much right now, I can't put one more thing on top. We need to know who this Skye girl is."

"Lisbeth is working as hard as she can."

"I don't doubt it. I'm also not able to leave, just FYI. If I do, they won't let me back in. And I still need to get the letter from him."

"I'm managing things on this end. Don't worry."

"Did Captain Bacote file everything?"

"Yes," comes a voice from across the room. I glance up to see the captain walking in. "I did."

FORTY-THREE

Friday, 6:45 p.m.

RYLAN SAYS, "I keep hearing things I didn't hear before."

"Like?"

"The fluorescent lights buzzing." He looks up at them. "Can you hear them?"

"I can't, no."

Anxiously, his leg bounces. Through the Plexiglas, I can't see it, but it makes his upper body vibrate. "It's the adrenaline. Will you stay here talking to me as long as you can? Otherwise, they'll send me back to my cell."

"Okay."

"Thanks." He licks his dry lips. "They asked me what I wanted for my last meal."

Outwardly, I force calmness. Inwardly, I feel every bit of the anxiety Rylan demonstrates. "What did you ask for?"

"Lasagna with garlic bread and a Caesar salad."

"That sounds good."

Though it's warm in here, he rubs his hands up and

down his arms. "I hope they enjoy it because I sure as hell won't be able to eat it."

"Maybe a bite or two," I say like it even matters.

"'The practice of injecting one or more drugs into a person for the express purpose of causing rapid death.'" He huffs an unamused laugh. "That's what Wikipedia says about lethal injection. I looked it up."

Down by my side, my fingernails dig into the palms of my hands. "Tell me your favorite memory of Mackenzie."

For one long beat, he stops bouncing his leg. His body quiets. "Her giggle was the best. Infectious is a good way to describe it. She was a chubby little toddler. I loved holding her down and tickling her belly. She'd roll around and laugh and laugh." His mouth curves pleasantly with the memory. "Yeah...best giggle ever."

For a long beat, my body quiets right along with his. I get lost in the memory, imagining him laughing as Destiny rolled around on the carpet giggling so hard she probably peed her diaper.

I wonder if my father ever did that with me.

Before I left the station to come here, I made a copy of Destiny's license and cut out just her face. I remember it now and take it from my pocket. I unfold it and hold it up to the Plexiglass. Rylan brightens. He leans in. He chuckles. "What is she thinking with that hair and nose ring?"

I smile. "She's pretty. She has your eyes."

He keeps staring at it. I keep it held up.

Gradually, Rylan's happiness fades. He glances up at the clock hanging behind me. His chest rises with a deep breath. He sits back. His leg resumes bouncing. I put the photo away.

He says, "I have to wear a diaper. They'll give me three needles. First is the sedative. The second paralyzes. The third stops my heart. I'll be restrained nearly thirty minutes before that with an IV of saline. I'll probably piss myself during those thirty minutes. Hell, I'll probably crap myself too. Between needles two and three, I'll be aware I'm not breathing. But I won't be able to react. If I haven't already crapped myself, this is when I will. My muscles will cramp. Then, my brain will die."

I'm aware I'm not breathing.

He keeps going, "Before needle one, I'll be allowed to say my last words. I don't know if I will. I doubt it. There'll be a spiritual advisor. They asked me who I wanted. I didn't care. They gave me a priest. I mean, if it were you, would you care?"

I take my first breath. My throat is raw and dry when I speak. "No."

"If the person I killed had family members coming, they'd be put in a separate room. That's a moot point in this case. The actual viewing of me will only be ten minutes if that. They won't show all the 'fun' behind-the-scenes things. The media will be there. I heard Bacote's coming."

"H-he's here already."

"Afterward, a spiritual advisor will be available for healing and trauma support," he says in a conversational tone like he's talking about the weather outside and not his upcoming death.

The guard opens the door. "Let's go, Rylan. Time for your lasagna."

He stands, looking at me through the thick Plexiglas. "Will you come back and keep talking to me?"

I swallow. "Yes."

FORTY-FOUR

Friday, 8 p.m.

IN THE WAITING ROOM, a guard approaches. He hands me an unsealed white envelope. "For Rylan's daughter."

My hands are unsteady when I take it.

The guard walks away.

I don't know how long I stand here staring at this envelope, but I'm sure as hell not reading the letter. Not right now at least.

My phone rings. It's Vaughn. Just seeing his name relaxes me. "Hey," I say, my mouth dry.

"Checking in. How are you holding up?"

I try to swallow but I have no saliva. On the other side of the waiting room sits Captain Bacote and one person from the local media. That's it. Two people in total to witness Rylan's last breath. "I'm going to be sick," I whisper.

"You're okay. Stay on the phone with me. Close your eyes. Center yourself. Breathe."

I do.

Weird enough, I hear the fluorescent bulbs. It's impossible, but I swear I smell the lasagna.

"I wish I was there with you," Vaughn says.

"Yeah." I turn away from the captain and the reporter. "Anything on Skye? Anything on the stay?"

"Nothing yet."

My voice comes quiet. "Do you think we'll get it?"

"I hope so."

FORTY-FIVE

Friday, 8:45 p.m.

"DID you know I wasn't there when Mackenzie was born?"
Rylan asks. "I was working. I didn't even know Cathy was
in labor."

Somewhere between my last visit and this one, they
cranked on the air. It's freezing in here. Yet, a bead of sweat
trails the side of his face. I watch it until it disappears under
his chin.

"Paige was there. She gave me all the details. So many
details that I felt as if I was there as well." His gaze flits to
the clock hanging over my shoulder.

I don't need to look to know that we have one more hour
until they take him away for good.

"Did you enjoy the lasagna?" I ask, knowing what a
stupid freaking question that is.

"Tell me about your family," he says, instead of
answering my asinine query.

A tremor runs through my body. Rylan notices.

"I'm sorry," I mumble.

"It's okay. Tell me about your family."

"Um...my family." *Focus, Nell, focus.* "My brother, Tyler, I'm raising him. Mom was incarcerated, so I'm his guardian."

"Is she still in?"

"She spent seven years locked up, but she's out now." I don't tell people my personal shit, yet somehow it spills from me. "Tyler's a teenager. We live in our grandfather's old house. But I have a feeling that's about to change."

"Why is that?"

"My estranged father just walked back into our lives. He proposed to my mother and she said yes. He wants the whole family to move back to Georgia. That's where the two of them met."

"What do you think about that?"

"Well, my brother wants to. He's my world, so I'll probably go. But—" I shrug— "I'm waiting for the other shoe to fall, or however the saying goes."

"Waiting for the other shoe to drop. And why is that?"

"It's my father's M-O. He's not exactly reliable. He's in my life, out, in, but mostly out."

"Everyone deserves a second chance, your father included."

Everyone deserves a second chance. I've heard that many times before. It usually goes in one ear and right out the other. But now, at this moment, it sticks. This man is about to die and those are his words to me. *Everyone deserves a second chance.*

We talk some more about my life, his, travel, food, and various other things. I even manage to forget I'm conversing with a man who is set to soon die. Every once in a while I glance over to the door that leads into the waiting room, willing Captain Bacote to appear and tell us the stay has been granted.

But the door stays fully closed.

Eventually, time is up.

The guard opens the entry on Rylan's side of our small room. He stands and puts his arms behind his back. The guard cuffs him.

"Would you be there for me?" Rylan quietly asks.

"What, in the room?"

"Yeah, in the room."

One very long moment creeps by. The guard doesn't move. Rylan doesn't move. *I* don't move. I don't think any of us even breathe. Somewhere deep in the crevices of my brain, I was expecting that question. I was hoping it wouldn't be asked, but I was expecting it.

Vaughn's words come back to me. *Rylan's going to look out though and see a comforting face.*

My legs wobble as I come to my feet. How is he so steady? "Yes, I'll be there."

With a nod, Rylan and the guard leave.

On my side of the Plexiglas, the waiting room door opens. I whip around, hope surging through me. My heart suspends beating. One look at Captain Bacote's face tells me the answer.

"*No.*"

He shakes his head.

"No!"

I lose it. My scream echoes off the walls. It knifes through the air. My heart beats so roughly it stabs the inside of my chest wall. My breaths come quickly. Too quickly.

My fingers curl into a fist. I look for anything to punch and end up slamming my knuckles into the Plexiglas.

Once. Twice.

And I keep punching and slapping until a smear of blood appears and a guard makes me leave.

FORTY-SIX

Friday, 11:54 p.m.

I NOW SIT in the viewing room with Captain Bacote on my left and a male reporter on my right. Three people total. That's it. The remaining seven chairs are empty. Straight ahead a heavy blue curtain covers a glass pane.

I'll be restrained nearly thirty minutes before that with an IV of saline. I'll probably piss myself during those thirty minutes. Hell, I'll probably crap myself too.

My gaze darts to the clock. In under a minute that curtain will open. I'll come face-to-face with Rylan. I draw in a deep breath, blowing it out slowly.

Captain Bacote leans in. "You okay?"

What an idiotic question. *No, I'm not okay.* I'm about to watch an innocent man be executed. To the right of me, the reporter waits, a notepad and pen in his lap. He's calm. Almost bored. How many of these does he go to, I wonder.

The curtain opens. My heart stops. Dressed in all white and with an IV in his arm, Rylan's strapped to a table that is propped up at an angle. In the room with him are the warden, a guard, a doctor, and a priest.

I have to wear a diaper.

It's a ridiculous thought, but I hope he didn't lose his bowels. I hope he has at least that final dignity to hold onto.

The practice of injecting one or more drugs into a person for the express purpose of causing rapid death.

On a silver table next to the IV stand are three syringes. My eyes go from them to Rylan's. He's looking right at me. I *will* maintain eye contact with him from here on out.

In my periphery, I see a phone on the wall. The warden checks the time.

Then he looks through the glass at the three of us. "Let me remind you photography is not permitted and you are required to remain silent throughout. There will be no entering or exiting until this is completed. Upon pronouncement of death, you will be escorted back to the waiting room to collect your belongings."

The warden turns to Rylan. "Rylan Scott, be it known you have pled guilty for the crime of murder in the first degree of Paige Bell. I am hereby authorized to cause the sentence of death to be executed upon you at this time. Would you like to make a final statement, Mr. Scott?"

Rylan's body trembles. "Just...just get it over with."

My hands fist so tightly I feel the strain in my neck.

The warden nods to the guard. He lowers the table. I keep my gaze fastened on Rylan's until I no longer can.

The warden glances at the clock. He stares at it until it ticks down. When it does, he nods to the doctor.

The doctor picks up the first syringe. He connects it to the hub of Rylan's IV line. Slowly, he pushes the medication in.

First is the sedative.

Rylan's eyes flutter close. I'm not a person who prays, but I do now that he's disappearing into that memory of tickling his daughter.

His body stops trembling.

Once the sedation syringe is empty, the doctor places it back on the tray and picks up number two.

The second paralyzes.

The doctor repeats, connecting the syringe to the hub and slowly pushing the medication in. Once it's empty, he places the syringe back on the tray. He picks up number three.

Between needles two and three, I'll be aware I'm not breathing. But I won't be able to react. If I haven't already crapped myself, this is when I will. My muscles will cramp. Then, my brain will die.

Like earlier, I realize I'm not breathing. My mouth opens. I draw in a breath. My heart thumps in my fingers, my neck, and through every vein intricately weaving through my body. It reminds me that I'm alive.

The doctor connects the last syringe. Slowly, he pushes the liquid in.

The third stops my heart.

FORTY-SEVEN

Saturday, 7 a.m.

I RUN FASTER than I've ever run before. My long legs eat up the trail. My lungs burn. Sweat drips. My vision warbles.

Still, I push harder.

I pass one trail runner. Then another. And another. The seconds tick to minutes. I erupt from the trail into a grassy meadow. I come to an abrupt stop. A large white pine stands alone, towering fifty feet into the air. I've seen this pine many times and have run past it with barely a look.

This time I walk to it. My chest rises and falls with heavy breaths. I step into its shadow. I reach up. Slowly I run my fingers across the stiff green needles.

It feels like life.

WHEN I PULL into my driveway, Vaughn's leaning up against his Mini Cooper checking his phone. He's already talking when I step from my SUV. "You don't answer your texts. You don't return your voicemails. What's a partner to think?"

"Sorry. I needed to clear my head." I walk toward my house. "You could've waited inside."

"I knocked. No one answered."

"Tyler was here when I left to go running." Inside, I find a note taped to the refrigerator. *Went to Starbucks with Dad to visit Mom.*

I open the door, grabbing two water bottles. I give one to Vaughn.

"How are you doing?" he asks.

"Okay, I guess."

Silently, we both drink.

He sits at my kitchen table. "Want to talk about it?"

"No." I take the seat across from him.

"I'm an asshole," he says.

"Vaughn, my friend, you are anything but that. Why would you say that?"

"I snapped at Charlotte last night. I was hovering over Lisbeth, hoping for results on Skye when Charlotte called me. She was being her usual sweet self just checking on me, and I took my frustration out on her. We were in that window, waiting to hear back on the stay, waiting for anything on Skye... and I lost it."

I drink more water. "It happens. Call her today, or go see her. Apologize."

"I will. She did not deserve my stress." He fiddles with the cap of his bottle. "Sometimes I think cops are meant to be alone."

"That's not true." Though I have thought those exact words myself.

"What, we can be different?"

I toast my water bottle to his. "Damn straight."

He sips, pondering me.

"What?"

"We know for a fact Twitch didn't do Paige. But he's going down for Cathy. Are you content with the arrest?"

"Hell no, I'm not content. Rylan went down for Paige. Twitch is going down for Cathy. A job well done most would say. Yet I am far beyond satisfied. I'm confident the same person did both women. I feel it in my gut. I don't want to close the case, but Owens expects us to."

"I was looking at your grandfather's boxes that you're storing at my place. There are a lot of files in those boxes. I didn't look through them, but please tell me they're not all cold cases. I'm not sure I can keep doing this job if so many cases go unsolved."

"The majority of those files are my grandfather's notes and thoughts. Things he didn't want to be filed officially. I'd say there are maybe twenty cold cases he never solved. He was a cop for a very long time. That's a pretty good solve rate."

"Maybe you and I need to start a box of our own. This will be our first one. Though technically it's an extension of your grandfather's."

We share a resigned smile.

"Okay, rolling with this," he says. "How did Twitch get that picture of Cathy's stabbed body? Did he come across her on the trail and take the photo? Did he find the picture in the garbage? He's adamant that he's never seen it before. He's been arrested for murder. Now would be the time to admit if he'd taken it himself or found it. Therefore—"

"Someone planted it on him. Just like someone put the knife in his things."

"I can't believe I'm rallying behind Twitch."

"He needs to go down for about a million things, but not this."

Vaughn's phone gets a text. So does mine, but it's on the other side of the room.

"No way." He stands, and as he walks toward my front door he says, "Lisbeth finally figured out who Skye is."

FORTY-EIGHT

Saturday, 8 a.m.

AFTER A QUICK SHOWER, I drive to the station. In the lobby, I make a brief stop at the receptionist's desk. She visibly cringes when she looks up and sees me.

"Don't you work the afternoon/evening shift?" I ask.

"Yes. I need the money. I took extra hours."

This makes me feel even worse. I get right to the point. "I was a dick to you yesterday. I'm sorry."

"I'll do better."

"You're doing just fine. Know that I'm a very hands-on detective. If anything comes in for me, make sure I get it."

"Got it." She nods.

"Thank you."

When I walk through the security door that leads to the back, I run straight into Sheriff Owens. He does not look happy to see me.

"What's wrong?" I ask.

"Well, for starters, Sergeant Rogers is not filing a formal complaint."

"Okay." I shrug. "Isn't that good news?"

"He said he's old school. 'Cops don't rat on cops,' were his exact words."

"Yeah, and?"

"And it doesn't matter, Nell. You're still suspended. The whole station witnessed you punch him. That can't go unpunished."

"And what about everything he's thrown my way?"

"Would you like to file a complaint?"

I resist the urge to roll my eyes. "No. When does my suspension start?"

"You're very unaffected by all of this."

"Because I am. Rogers is an asshole."

His lips press tightly. His head shakes. He studies me.

I don't have time for this, but I stand here, waiting.

"I don't know what to do with you. Wrap up all the paperwork on Cathy and Twitch, then I don't want to see you back here for two weeks. Unpaid."

I should be irritated, annoyed, hell, even furious, but somehow, I'm not. I'm simply indifferent. "Fine."

Owens lowers his voice. "Rogers wasn't wrong. I do show you favoritism. That has to stop. It's not good for either one of our careers. You understand?"

"I do." I look past his shoulder and into the workroom. I spy Rogers sitting at his desk, staring at me. His nose looks fine. I wish it didn't. "I'm not apologizing if that's what you expect."

"I didn't say that, did I?"

"No, you didn't."

"Nell!" From across the room, Vaughn waves me over.

"Go on," Owens says. "Finish up."

At the IT desk, Lisbeth has a picture on her screen of a young teenage girl with long straight auburn hair, deep blue eyes, very little makeup, and dressed in a private school uniform. "I was just telling Detective London how sorry I was I didn't figure this out sooner. I've been working around the clock. I promise you I have."

"We know. What have you found?

"Her name was Skye Oliver. Her body was found in a dumpster in Knoxville. She'd been dead three days. Overdosed on a cocktail of things—heroine, coke, alcohol. This happened the week before Paige Bell was murdered. Skye was the daughter of one of Knoxville's wealthiest men."

Lisbeth clicks on a new picture, bringing up a family photo taken from a Knoxville paper. It shows Skye standing in front of her parents, all dressed formally for a fundraising event. Other people are in the photo as well. Lisbeth points to each. "Captain Bacote and his wife, the mayor, a commissioner, and this one is Preacher Mitch's brother who later becomes chief of police."

I lean in, studying Skye's parents.

It's been ten years, but I point as I look up at my partner. "Recognize that person?"

He squints. "Ah, damn."

"Keep this to yourself," I tell Lisbeth. "No one knows anything until we're sure."

FORTY-NINE

Saturday, 10:15 a.m.

WITH HER EVER-PRESENT backpack fuller than usual, Rebecca cuts across Wal-Mart's parking lot. I pull in, slowly trailing behind her.

After a few seconds, she glances over her shoulder, frowning when she realizes it's us.

Vaughn's already opening his door before I put my vehicle in park.

She looks between us. "Everything okay?"

"Where are you going?" my partner asks.

"Like I said, moving on." She shrugs. "Nothing for me here anymore. Glad to hear you arrested Twitch. Glad to hear Cathy's murder will be avenged."

"You manipulated us," Vaughn says, his tone much calmer than I expect. "Your name is Rebecca Oliver. Ten years ago, you were married to Henry and you had a daughter, Skye. You lived in Knoxville. Your husband made a fortune in real estate. Fast-forward a decade and here you are homeless with a daughter who overdosed and a husband who committed suicide."

Rebecca doesn't blink, doesn't shrug, doesn't do anything. She simply keeps looking at Vaughn.

I say, "Your daughter got mixed up with Cathy. Those pornos made her big money where you and your husband were concerned. You were a bottomless blackmail pit when it came to Skye. First, came her death. Found in a dumpster like discarded trash. Within days your husband caves. He can't take it. He commits suicide. Then you lose it. You decide vigilante justice is the way to go. You knock on Cathy's door, and her sister opens it. They're identical twins, you didn't know. You stabbed the wrong sister."

Rebecca still does not comment. No movement. She doesn't even swallow.

Vaughn says, "You planted the knife in Rylan Scott's truck. Thanks to your close friendship with Captain Bacote, you were able to keep tabs on the case. That's when you discovered that you killed Paige, not Cathy, and that a nine-year-old girl witnessed the whole thing. Hell, he probably even told you where to find Cathy once you were ready to finish the job. But why wait? You and Cathy have been 'friends' for a long time. Why wait until now to carry out your sentence on her?"

Rebecca continues to remain silent.

Folding my arms, I study her, working through everything. "Because you figured Cathy was the key to finding Destiny. No one knew where she was, not even your good friend Captain Bacote." I hold a hand up. "Now I'm not saying he knew what you were doing, but you certainly used his knowledge of the case."

Still, nothing from Rebecca.

"Rylan went down for Paige. With Twitch being the

asshole he is, he makes an excellent fall guy for Cathy. You planted that knife and that photo." Vaughn cocks his head. "How pissed are you that Destiny committed suicide? What were your plans with her? Another violent stabbing?"

"Eye for an eye," I say. "Her whole family for yours. Was it a coincidence it all happened the same week, just like your family? Or was it planned? Probably a little of both. You didn't realize Cathy would see her daughter right here in our little county. But she did. And it all started to click into place."

Finally, Rebecca says something. "You can't prove any of this."

"Let me see your right arm," I demand.

"I'm not letting you see my right arm." Her chin lifts.

I step forward. "You can either let us see your arm on your own or we will slam you into this pavement and rip your sleeve off. What's it going to be?"

"You wouldn't do that."

"Oh. Yes. I would."

She hesitates, and I visualize the wheels turning. She doesn't know about the one piece of evidence that will link her to this. Vaughn and I stay rooted to our spots, staring her down, ready if she sprints. She's weighing that out as well. She knows if she runs, we will catch her without an issue.

Her chest lifts and falls with a heavy breath. The backpack slides from her shoulders. Her oversized tee hangs past her elbows. She pushes up the sleeve, revealing a row of X's circling her upper right arm. "It means not to mess with me. I got it a very long time ago."

"We know what it means," I say. "Your daughter had the same one."

"She did?"

Skye was unhappy. She ran from home. She may have

hated her mom, but something about that tattoo carried with her.

Rebecca swallows. The shirt sleeve falls back into place. Her eyes swim with tears. "I never knew..."

"Destiny. Rylan. Paige. Cathy." The names punch into me. "All dead because of you."

"Skye. Henry. Dead because of Cathy." Rebecca straightens. "Avenged because of me."

FIFTY

STANDING BESIDE ME, Captain Bacote stares through the two-way mirror at Rebecca sitting in the interrogation room.

"I haven't seen Rebecca in years," he says. "I didn't realize she was in this area. My wife used to check on her now and again. Then one day she told me Rebecca's number had been disconnected and the house they lived in had been sold. I figured she moved somewhere where no one knew her to get a fresh start. I never imagined this would be her." He nods toward the mirror. "Boy, does she look different."

"I suppose living homeless for years on end will make anyone look different," I say.

Bacote glances over at me. "This is unbelievable. Our families used to do barbecues. Henry and I were on a bowling league together."

"Did they come to you when they were blackmailed?" I ask.

"Yes. I had a little talk with Natalie, or rather Cathy. I threatened her. She was a piece of work. My threat fell on deaf ears. She didn't care. A few months later everything happened with Paige's stabbing. All fingers pointed to Rylan. I regretted bringing your grandfather in. All he did was add more doubt to a case I needed closed. We found the murder weapon. It's not the like the Scotts were some upstanding couple. They were trash. I had enough to put Rylan away. I certainly never thought the real killer was Rebecca Oliver."

My respect for the captain has continuously fluctuated since video chatting with him. Now it's completely gone. "Trash or not, an entire family has been wiped out. Rylan had his faults, but he was a good man. Doubt is not your enemy. It's there for a reason. You should've listened. Look at everything that's happened because you didn't."

With that, I walk out.

FIFTY-ONE

Sunday, 6 p.m.

I STAND beside Vaughn at the tracks where Destiny ran headfirst into the train. From the envelope the guard gave me, I take out the letter that Rylan wrote. I'm nervous as I unfold it and begin to read aloud:

Mackenzie,

As I sit down to write this, I'm reminded of the first day I held you in my arms. I promised myself that I would not let anything happen to you. You may blame me for all that has transpired, but for me, your safety was above everything else.

My life changed the day you were born. I never knew my heart could beat for someone and that I would start caring for you and your future.

I want to tell you that I love you from the bottom of my heart. You may not know, but you are the reason why I smiled every single day.

If there is a tomorrow when we're not together, there is something you must always remember: you are braver than you believe, stronger than you seem, and smarter than you think.

Life is not always fair and square; you will have proud moments as well as not-so-proud ones. The key to happiness is to stay humble, live truthfully, learn from mistakes, and try not to make them again. And when you're not sure if you are doing the right thing or are on the right path, trust your intuition. It will guide you down the correct path.

But the most important thing is... even if we're apart, I'll always be with you.

Love,

Daddy

My emotions rob the last few lines from being said. Vaughn speaks them for me. When he finishes, he hands me a lighter. I flick it and touch the bottom left corner. Together, we watch the paper curl and turn black, then flash with the growing flame.

The wind kicks up. I release it. It drifts across the tracks, scattering ashes in its journey. Eventually, there is nothing left.

Vaughn shifts, putting his arm around me. I lay my head against him. We stay very silent and still for a long while.

Then we turn to walk back to his Mini Cooper.

"I'm leaving," I tell him.

"Only two weeks. You'll be back."

"No. I'm leaving. For good."

Vaughn stops walking. He takes his Ray-Bans off to look at me.

"Mom's parole officer approved the paperwork," I say. "She'll finish probation in Georgia. Tyler wants to go. I plan on putting my grandfather's house up for sale. I'll get a place of my own in Georgia, near my parents. Tyler will have all of us nearby. It'll be good for him. And me. Mom too. There are a lot of bad memories for her in this area.

"I'm going to take time off. I need to think about the next steps. Because I'm not sure this is the right career. Once upon a time I wanted to join the military. Maybe I will now. Or go back to school for my master's. I don't know. But what I do know is that I haven't been making good decisions. And that bothers me. I don't like being Sheriff Brach's legacy."

"What about your father?"

"Everyone deserves a second chance," I repeat back Rylan's words.

"Well, this news sucks."

Playfully, I punch his shoulder. "You'll be fine."

He pulls me in for a hug. I'm not sure how long we stand, tightly gripping each other, but when we pull away both of us have tears in our eyes.

With a sniff, I wipe mine. "It's not like I'm dying. I'm simply moving to Georgia. You can visit, *Sergeant* London. Congratulations by the way."

"Thanks." He grins. "Want to celebrate my promotion?"

"Hell, yeah."

We finish walking to the car. He opens the driver's side, but he doesn't get in. Instead, he looks at me over the top.

"What?" I ask.

"Did I ever tell you I'm a little psychic?" He pinches his thumb and index finger together. "Just a little."

"And?" I laugh.

"And... I say you'll be back."

OTHER BOOKS BY S. E. GREEN

The Lady Next Door

The Family

Sister Sister

The Strangler

The Suicide Killer

Monster

The Third Son

Vanquished

Mother May I

Ultimate Sacrifice

Silence

ABOUT THE AUTHOR

S. E. Green is the award-winning, best-selling author of young adult and adult fiction. She grew up in Tennessee where she dreaded all things reading and writing. She didn't read her first book for enjoyment until she was twenty-five. After that, she was hooked! When she's not writing, she loves traveling and hanging out with a rogue armadillo that frequents her coastal Florida home.

Printed in Dunstable, United Kingdom